A Girls Guide to School

Sharon Witt
M.Ed.

Girl Wise ®
A Girls Guide to School
Book 5 in the Girl Wise series

September 2020
Reprinted August 2023
Reprinted February 2024
Reprinted January 2025

Published by Collective Wisdom Publications Pty
Ltd PO Box 150
Mt Evelyn Victoria 3796
www.sharonwitt.com.au

A catalogue record for this
work is available from the
National Library of Australia

Design and cartoons: Ivan Smith, Communiqué Graphics, Lilydale
Printed in Australia by Openbook Howden

Inside

This book belongs
to an amazing girl!

You are a wonderful, creative, inspiring, strong, and talented girl!

You are AMAZING!

You may notice that I have added a couple of amazing co-authors in this book. Who better than a couple of **EXPERT GIRLS** who are right in the middle of their own primary school journey?

MILLIE and **MACKENZIE** will be adding their own helpful advice along the way too, so look out for their notes along the way (thanks Millie and Mac ☺).

Hopefully you will feel a **LOT** better after reading through this book. You may read it many times over as you move through primary school. Sometimes, you might simply pick up a chapter in the book to help you through a particular problem or challenge you may face.

Just remember, there are **MANY** people that are here to help you through your primary school years. You are never alone!

You are AMAZING ☺

Love **Sharon x**

Introducing my helpful co-authors!

Meet Millie

Hi girls! My name is Millie, and I am 8 years old and in Grade 3 this year at school. I'm excited to be a part of this book and give you some helpful advice for school. Here is a little more about me.

Favourite hobbies

I like to dance, have movie marathons with the author of this book (Sharon ☺), work in my slime lab (which used to be my kitchen cubby house, and which I have just renovated and made MUCH better). I enjoy cooking and making crazy things like edible slime.

I also enjoy playing in the pool, singing, and playing with my friends.

Best thing I like about school

I enjoy having fun with my friends and eating lunch.

Best memory so far of primary school

Probably being with my best friend Grace in the same class. (She's my ultimate best friend!)

Favourite food

Definitely popcorn! I also love mango, edible slime ☺, avocado, tacos, pasta carbonara and cheese toasties.

Favourite subject at school

My favourite subject at school is art.
I have won some school awards with my art.

Best holiday I've been on

I've been on lots of holidays with my family. Every single one was fun so I can't decide. Some favourites have been travelling to New Zealand and America.

Favourite movies

Ooooh! That's a tough one because I LOVE movies so much. Some favourites would have to be *Maleficent 2*, the *Pitch Perfect* movies and *Paddington 2*.

If I were an animal, I'd like to be a...

Dolphin. I'd like to be a trained dolphin (like the ones at Sea World) so I can do cool tricks.

Introducing my helpful co-authors!

Meet Mackenzie

My name is Mackenzie. I am 11 years old and in Grade 5 this year. I have been in primary school for a few years now, so I hope some of my advice will help you out. I am at my second school having changed in Grade 3.

Favourite hobbies

My favourite hobbies are cheerleading, art, and dance. I also enjoy photography.

Best thing I like about school

The best thing about primary school is getting to see and play with my friends and my teachers. I also enjoy going on school camps. I have been on two already, and I'm about to go on my third.

Best memory so far of primary school

My favourite memories of primary school so far would be making new friends after I changed primary schools.

I also really enjoy the school discos. We have them every year.

Favourite food

I would have to say that my favourite foods are anything sugary. ☺ If I have to choose healthy foods, I would say that I love my mum's homemade pesto pasta.

Favourite subject at school

My favourite subjects at school are maths and Italian because I really enjoy learning different languages. In maths, I enjoy solving problems.

Best holiday I've been on

My favourite holiday was travelling to California in America. My mum and dad used to live there so I travelled back there for a visit.

Favourite television show

My favourite is definitely *Friends*. I like to watch an episode (or sometimes three ☺) every night.

If I were an animal, I'd like to be a…

Butterfly, because they can fly anywhere they want, and they look beautiful too.

A new adventure begins

The school year awaits you
A great place to be
Who will you meet?
Who will you see?
Whatever you make of it
You get to decide
To learn and discover
You're in for a ride!
Make sure you ask questions
Be adventurous and seek
To discover new things
Every day, every week
This is your new adventure
Yes it is true
To learn all you can
This year is for you

What are you most looking forward to at school this year?

I am excited to learn new things.

STARTING SCHOOL

Starting school

I still remember my very first day of primary school.

I was exactly four years and nine months old and I was **VERY** ready to begin the new adventure of school. I couldn't wait to meet my first teacher and go and buy my first ever school bag, lunch box and pencil case. I also knew that some of my friends from kindergarten would also be joining me at my new school. Imagine spending five days in a row with a whole bunch of friends. That sounded exciting to me!

And it was. For the most part, my seven years at primary school were very **HAPPY**, full of **LAUGHTER**, lots of **LEARNING** and new **ADVENTURES**. My best memories were of playing with friends outside at recess, wearing my favourite stripy coloured tights (I was VERY cool!), making many artistic creations, including a panelled window made from different coloured cellophane, and of course, day trips to many places, including the zoo and the museum.

If you are about to start school for the very first time, you may be feeling excited, or a bit **NERVOUS** (like you have one thousand butterflies in your tummy!) maybe **WORRIED** about what it will be like, or very **HAPPY** and prepared because you have been waiting for this moment for what seems like a **LONG** time.

Perhaps you are worried about getting to know lots of new people, scared that other girls might not talk to you, or who will you play with at recess.

But **TRY NOT TO WORRY**. Everyone has to begin school at some stage; your mum, dad, grandma, grandpa, aunts, uncles, or your big sister or brother have **ALL** started school at some point.

And guess what?

They got through it!

And you know another thing about school? The more you go to school, the more **FAMILIAR** it becomes, and the more comfortable you will be.

Millie says ...

When I started school for the first time, I was very, very **NERVOUS!**

I was already at the school at 'Littlies', which is pre-school. But I hadn't met my prep teacher until just before Christmas, before the school holidays. I wasn't very excited about starting school because I didn't know what it would be like, so I cried and cried for about two hours the day before.

Once I got there on my first day, I cried for about half an hour because I was **WORRIED** and **NERVOUS**, but then I had so much fun during the day, that when my parents came to pick me up at the end of the day, I didn't want to go home.

It really only took me about three days to settle in and get to know my teacher. I loved her. She is still one of my favourite teachers.

Mackenzie says ...

When I was first starting school, I was really **EXCITED**, and I absolutely loved the name badges that we were given to wear because we would know everyone's name. I also had lots of friends from kindergarten that moved across to the same primary school as me, so that was great. I wasn't scared or upset on my first day. In fact, I was very excited to begin school.

I was comfortable because I had some very good friends starting with me, so that made it much easier.

Ideas from...

'The best thing about primary school for me is getting homework.'

Sophie, aged 7

'My favourite thing about primary school is that I'm happy that the work isn't too hard and the teachers aren't too strict. My favourite subjects are maths, physical education and art.'

Tara, aged 8

'What I enjoy most about school is spending time with my friends. I also enjoy art and performing arts because I love to use my imagination.'

Isla, aged 9

'I love not having to change classrooms everyday like they do in high school, and I have a great group of friends.'

Lacey, aged 9

'I like learning new things and doing fun activities with my classmates.'

Hannah, aged 10

'The best thing about school is having good friends, and I enjoy learning.'

Abi, aged 10

'One of my favourite things about school is art lessons.'

Matilda, aged 10

Ideas from...

'My favourite thing about being in primary school is you get to do lots of different classes. My favourite is art.'

Jasmine, aged 7

'What I enjoy most about school is that you get to make friends.'

Karlee, aged 9

My favourite thing about primary school is probably that it is not so strict as a high school, and you don't have as many rules. It's fun.

Nevie, aged 10

My favourite thing about school is going to the library because I like reading. I also enjoy playing with my friends and practising spelling.

Charlie, aged 7

'The best thing about school is seeing my friends every day and playing on the equipment outside.'

Shiloh, aged 6

'One of my favourite things about school is getting to do art.'

Isabelle, aged 6

Coping with change

Change sometimes causes us to WORRY a bit. Perhaps you have already experienced changes in your life.

You might have:

- Moved house
- Changed schools
- Had a new baby join your family
- A change in your family circumstances
- Moved interstate
- Lost a pet ☹

However you are feeling right now, remember that you have lots of SUPPORT to help you start school well and SETTLE IN comfortably. You don't have to worry about learning everything straight away either! You will have plenty of TIME to learn things like where the toilets are, where the playground is, what time playtime and lunch are, and what your day will look like.

Your class teacher is there to help you, listen to what you have to say, and will answer any questions you have along the way.

Don't forget! It's more than okay to ask **QUESTIONS**. That's how you will find out what to do or where something is.

Over your many years at school, you will learn to ask **MANY** questions. That's how you learn new things.

The good news is, you are **NEVER ALONE**.

There are always adults (like your parents) who will be in your life every step of the way.

Are you ready to find out more about what to expect at school?

Okay, then let's read ahead! ☺

Beginning a new school year

Perhaps you are about to begin your very **FIRST** year at school (sometimes known as Prep, Reception or Foundation) depending on where you live. Or maybe you have already been at school for a year or more.

However, each year is a new beginning at school. Over the Christmas break, you will have quite a few weeks off school.

This could be anywhere from five to seven weeks depending on which school you attend.

It is a good thing to have a break from school at the end of the year. You have worked hard and used your brain a lot to learn many new things.

Each new year, you'll go into a **BRAND-NEW** grade or class. This is because you are a year older now. You may be in a class with some of your friends from last year, and you'll also have new children join your class.

It's a good thing to have new classmates because this is a wonderful opportunity to get to know new friends.

You might be feeling a bit **EXCITED** about beginning a new year at school and seeing your friends again. You most likely have a **NEW TEACHER** and are looking forward to being in their class.

Or you may be feeling nervous or worried or a little bit unsure about what to expect when you go back to school. Perhaps you didn't have the best experience at school last year and didn't find your days easy or enjoyable.

If that is the case, I want you to think about this for a moment.

You have a **BRAND-NEW**, never-to-be-repeated year ahead of you.

Write here about your first
day of school this year...

Write here about your first day of school this year...

A brand-new beginning

Last year has come and gone, and guess what? You got through it. If last year wasn't the best for you, try not to go into this new school year worrying about what has already gone.

You can begin a **BRAND-NEW** year with a **FRESH ATTITUDE**.

Imagine that it is going to be a great year at school. You are going to do your **VERY BEST**.

Perhaps you found it difficult to pay attention in class last year, or you found yourself being told to stop interrupting in class.

Maybe that left you feeling upset or frustrated.

You can make a decision to sit down at the front of the class, if possible, and decide to practise **LISTENING** more to your teacher and using **EYE CONTACT** so that they know you're listening.

Maybe you found it hard to learn your spelling words, or challenging to practise your reading. That is okay! Plenty of children find different things at school tricky. It may take some time for these things to become EASIER for you.

What I want you to do, as you begin a new year, is to FOCUS on the things that you CAN do already. For example, maybe you are an encouraging friend to others.

Or perhaps you are always very HELPFUL to your teacher, asking if there's anything you can do to help at the end of a class.

Do you keep your books and pencils NEAT and TIDY? Do you enjoy creating pieces of art? Maybe you find working with numbers easier than other students.

The point is, focus on the things that you CAN do, rather than the things that feel CHALLENGING.

We ALL have things that are harder for us than others. For example, I'm not brilliant at understanding maths and fractions, but I LOVE to write, and I REALLY enjoy talking with and making new friends.

So put on a BIG SMILE! Have a POSITIVE attitude, and let's get into it ☺.

Settling into a new school

If you have moved house recently or have had to move schools for any other reason, it can be scary to start again at a new school. We can feel nervous or worried – even excited – because we are **UNSURE** about what to expect.

'Will I make new friends easily?'
'Will I like my teachers, and will they like me?'
'Will I be able to find my way around the new school?'
'What if the work is much harder than I'm used to?'

These are all **NORMAL** questions to ponder when experiencing such a change.

Perhaps you know someone who already attends that school. Ask a parent to help organise a time to catch up with them. You might be able to ask your friend some questions about your new school.

Orientation Day

Before you start attending school every day, you will most likely go and have a **VISIT** at your new school for a half or full day. This will probably happen towards the end of the year before you start, leading up to the summer holidays.

This is called Orientation Day. On this day you will meet your teacher, make some new friends who are most likely going to be in your class next year, and **FAMILIARIZE** yourself with the school grounds. Sometimes when we are experiencing something brand new, for the first time, we can feel a little nervous. We may not know what to expect. (Hopefully this book helps ☺.) When we actually go and visit a new place or go with someone we trust, it can help us feel better about going the next time because it won't be so new each time.

Here are some things you might do on Orientation Day:

- Meet your teacher that you'll have next year
- Play some games
- Practise writing your name
- Play in the playground
- Listen to a story
- Go for a tour of the school
- Meet new friends
- Find out where you will put your schoolbag when you begin school
- Do some drawing or painting
- Eat your food

LET'S GET
ORGANISED

Getting prepared!

What you'll need for school

Your parents or caregiver will receive a notice from your new school that will explain all the items you will need to bring on your first day of school. Don't worry about this. They will help you get these ORGANIZED and LABELLED so you're ready to start.

So let's take a look at some of the items you may need for your very first day at school:

- School bag
- Stationery (books, pencil case)
- Lunch or healthy snacks (you may only attend half a day for the first week)
- Drink bottle
- Uniform

(Some primary schools have a UNIFORM and as part of this, they have a special school bag that has the school colours and logo on it.)

School bag

If you have been at school before now, you may still have a school bag. If not, you can have fun choosing a brand new one for the new school. However, many schools have a school bag as part of their school uniform. Make sure that you don't put too many books and other items in your school bag to make it TOO HEAVY – you need to ensure there isn't too much weight on your back and shoulders.

Lunch box

Choose a lunch box with a few different compartments if possible. This will help you to be able to include a variety of different foods such as fruit, cut-up vegetables, dips and sandwiches to keep your body and brain **WELL FED** throughout the school day.

A lunch box that also has a place to hold a small freezer brick is also helpful. That way, your lunch box will stay nice and cool through the warmer months.

Water bottle

You need to drink **LOTS** of water throughout the day to keep your mind and body active and working properly. If you don't like the taste of plain water too much, try adding a few drops of **LEMON** to your water (not cordial!). Avoid adding any sugary drinks to your water bottle – H_2O is the way to go!

TOP TIP

If you know ahead of time that the next day is going to be very warm at school, fill your water bottle up to the ¾ mark and no more, (as water expands when frozen) and store it in the freezer overnight. That way, during the day, as it begins to defrost, you'll have a nice, cold, icy drink. You can also place the cold water bottle on your forehead to cool yourself down when outside playing. ☺

School books

You will probably have quite a few school books at home that may need **COVERING** before you begin the new school year. Some girls like the plain contact over their books (which protects your books in case they get wet or have something spilt on them).

Others prefer to choose some bright or pattered contact, or **SPECIAL** book covers to personalize their books. For example, you may love animals or sports and might be able to find some book covers that have those images. Other girls like to cut out or print favourite pictures and cover their books with these. It may be worth checking with your school if they are happy for you to personalise your books with pictures and patterns (most teachers are ☺).

Don't try and cover your books in contact yourself. It is more difficult than you may realise. You might need mum, dad or another helpful adult to handle this job! You can now buy special slip covers which just slip onto your book to protect it.

LABEL EVERYTHING!!!!

Your name is **YOUR OWN**, and it is important to put your name on **EVERYTHING** that you are going to bring to school with you.

As careful as you may be, things do go missing, and other students 'may borrow' items without telling you (it happens ☹).

You can ask an adult to write your full name on all of your school items or you may even purchase some vinyl name stickers online that come in packets. Usually, there are lots of name stickers that you can attach to all your things.

Stationery

Many schools will provide you with the majority of the items you will need to use at school such as pencils, erasers, textas, rulers, etc. Some schools, on the other hand, will send home a **STATIONERY LIST** with items that your parents/caregivers will need to purchase for you.

You may need to purchase some of the following:

- Pencil case
- Pencil sharpener
- Eraser
- Coloured pencils
- Grey lead pencils
- Coloured textas
- Scissors
- Glue stick
- Ruler

Sun hat

This may already be part of your school uniform, depending on your primary school. Some schools **EXPECT** you to bring your own broad brim hat with you to school each day (or keep it in a special place in your classroom, such as your locker or tub). It is **VERY** important that you make sure you are being **SUN SMART** at school when you are playing outside and protect your head from the sun's harmful UV rays.

Uniform

Many schools will have a **SCHOOL UNIFORM** that all students are required to wear. If this is not your first year at school, you could try on last years' school uniform a few weeks before school goes back to make sure it fits!

If it's your very first year at school, make sure that you take the time to try on your brand-new uniform about two weeks before you begin school – just in case you've grown a bit more over the holidays. ☺

TAKE CARE OF YOUR UNIFORM!

When you get home from school, if your school uniform is still clean, make sure you **HANG IT UP** in your wardrobe or **FOLD IT NEATLY** and put it in your drawer or on the end of your bed.

Don't dump your clothes on your bedroom floor. If they are dirty, pop your uniform in your dirty clothes basket or in the laundry basket.

School shoes

Many schools will require you to have special school shoes (often black) to go with your school uniform. These shoes can be purchased from many stores. You will most likely go with a parent or caregiver and try them on to make sure they are **COMFORTABLE** and **FIT CORRECTLY**, and that you have room to grow! Don't get your school shoes too soon – you still may have some growing to do in the weeks before school goes back.

Some schools allow you to wear comfy sneakers or runners for school. As long as you can put your own shoes on and take them off yourself, you will be fine.

If you have shoes with **LACES**, you need to ask a helpful adult to teach you how to tie your own shoelaces. This will take some practice to get it right, but you'll pick it up in no time.

Some children find it easier to wear school shoes with **VELCRO**, which may make it easier for you to put on and remove your own shows.

Find what works best for you. ☺

Checklist for school supplies

- [ ] School bag
- [ ] School shoes
- [ ] Lunchbox
- [ ] Water bottle
- [ ] Stationery
- [ ] Pencil case
- [ ] School uniform

GETTING INTO A ROUTINE

Morning routine

Attending school five days a week can be TIRING and can take a lot of energy. You might wake up feeling a bit tired and sleepy first thing in the morning, so the more you can prepare the night before, the better.

Getting organized for school is also called a ROUTINE. This means that you plan to do the SAME things at a similar time each day or night.

You can sit down with your parents or caregiver to plan what you need to do to prepare for the new school day each morning.

For example:
What time will you wake up each school morning?
Will you pack your school bag the night before?
Where will you set out your uniform, ready to put on?

Whatever you decide with your parents, it can be a helpful idea to write out a CHECKLIST of things you need to remember to do each morning in order of what needs to be done. You don't want to forget to pack your sports shoes, or even worse, your lunchbox!

Ideas from...

'My advice is to lay out your uniform ready for school the next day. Also, put your lunch box on the kitchen bench and your drink bottle in the fridge ready to go.'

Isla, aged 9

'Make your lunch (or get an adult to do it) the night before school. I always put my uniform on as soon as I get up on school days.'

Sophie, aged 6

'Wake up early and have a good, healthy breakfast, and pack a healthy lunch box with something you like to eat.'

Karlee, aged 9

'I wake up in the morning and get dressed first into my school uniform. Then I eat some breakfast and watch a couple of cartoons. My mum helps pack my lunch and schoolbag because this is my first year at school.'

Shiloh, aged 6

'Each school morning I wake up, eat breakfast whilst watching something on youtube. I talk to my mum, get ready for school, and make sure I have everything for the day.'

Lacey, aged 9

'Try and do things quickly – and don't wake up on the wrong side of bed (so you're not grumpy). My morning schedule is: get out of bed, get dressed, have breakfast and brush my teeth.'

Jasmine, aged 7

'My advice is to get up at the same time each morning. Pack your school bag and get all ready for school before you play.'

Abi, aged 10

Ideas from...

'My advice is to stick to a routine, put out your uniform the night before and then, after breakfast, the clothes are all there ready.'

Grace, aged 9

'My morning routine is, I get up, get changed, eat my breakfast, brush my teeth, pack my lunchbox, and if I have library, I pack my library bag.'

Lexi, aged 8

'I like to have a routine for school. Firstly, I wake up and I go to the bathroom. Then I have a shower or bath, brush my teeth, make my bed, put on my uniform and have some breakfast. Routines make me feel way more organised. My best friend was having trouble getting to school on time, so I encouraged her to make a routine for herself. It made her feel much more organised, too.'

Charlotte, aged 11

'I like to get everything ready the night before so I can go to sleep knowing that I am ready. Then, when I wake up, it doesn't take too long to get ready.'

Nevie, aged 10

'Every morning I get up at 6:30am and get dressed into my uniform. Then I eat breakfast and brush my teeth. After that I make sure that I have everything I need and then I am off to school! On the way to school we tell jokes and funny stories with mum and my sister, Elyssa.'

Annabelle, aged 8

Millie says ...

First thing in the morning, I wake up and make my bed.

I then get dressed into my school uniform and then head downstairs and have my breakfast.

Then I make my sandwich, add it to my lunchbox with the rest of my snacks and put it in my school bag.

I then get my hair done, brush my teeth, and then I'm out the door.

Mackenzie says...

The first thing I do on a school morning is get up and get dressed by 8am. Then I have my breakfast. I usually eat cereal. I then do my hair and spray on some perfume (so I smell nice ☺). Then I brush my teeth, pack my school bag, and if it's a cool day, put my jumper on. Then I put my shoes and socks on, and I'm ready to go.

A typical morning routine may look like this...

MY MORNING SCHOOL ROUTINE

7AM Wake up

- [ ] Wash my face
- [ ] Make my bed
- [ ] Eat breakfast
- [ ] Put on school uniform for the day
- [ ] Put my lunch in school bag
- [ ] Put any school books in school bag
- [ ] Brush teeth
- [ ] Brush hair
- [ ] Put my shoes on
- [ ] Leave for school

Write a list of what your morning school routine looks like...

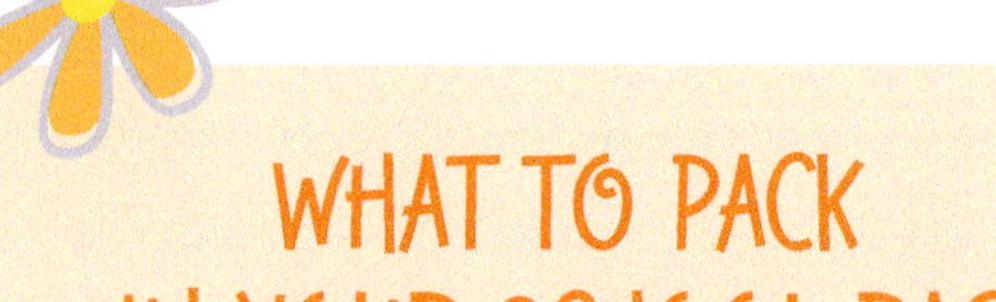

WHAT TO PACK IN YOUR SCHOOL BAG

- [ ] Lunch box

- [ ] Pencil case

- [ ] Water bottle

- [ ] Sunhat

- [ ] Reader and books

- [ ] Homework

- [ ] Sports clothes and shoes

What's in your school bag?

Write a list here of what you need to take to school.

Draw a picture of your school bag.

Things to leave at home

There are some items that I'm sure you would just love to bring to school with you. But there are some things that are far too precious or NOT APPROPRIATE to bring to school. These include things like an iPad, or other electronic devices. They should be left at home where they can be kept safe. Any items that are very important to you should be left at home.

Sometimes, you might want to bring in a special item especially for SHOW & TELL. That is okay, so long as you make a special arrangement with your parents. You could ask your teacher to put your special item away in a safe place at school until you need to get it out to show your classmates.

KEEPING
WELL

Eating well

School life is very busy, so, you will need to make sure that you take good care of your HEALTH. That includes making sure you eat well, drink lots of water, exercise and play, as well as getting a good night's sleep.

When we get the balance right, we should feel GOOD!

Sometimes, you might be feeling a little unwell, or catch a cold or need some extra sleep. But if you look after yourself, hopefully you won't get sick too often.

School life can be VERY tiring at times. You have to concentrate for periods of time, and are often very active. So, the FIRST thing you need to do each morning is make sure you eat a healthy breakfast! Your mind and body are much like a car, and need fuel to keep going throughout the day.

Some healthy breakfast ideas:

- Toast with spreads (like Vegemite, jam or honey)
- Fruit (blueberries are ESPECIALLY good brain food!)
- Weetbix (keep away from cereals with lots of sugar.)
- Yoghurt
- Pancakes
- A smoothie

Eating well at school

You are going to be using your brain a lot during the school day. And your body needs to stay **HYDRATED** and be given lots of **ENERGY** to make it work at its best. This means you need to drink **WATER** and eat lots of **HEALTHY FOODS** throughout the day.

It's important that you include healthy foods in your lunch box that are good for your growing mind and body. Try and avoid taking sugary foods and junk foods like chips and sweet biscuits. (Save them for special occasions ☺.)

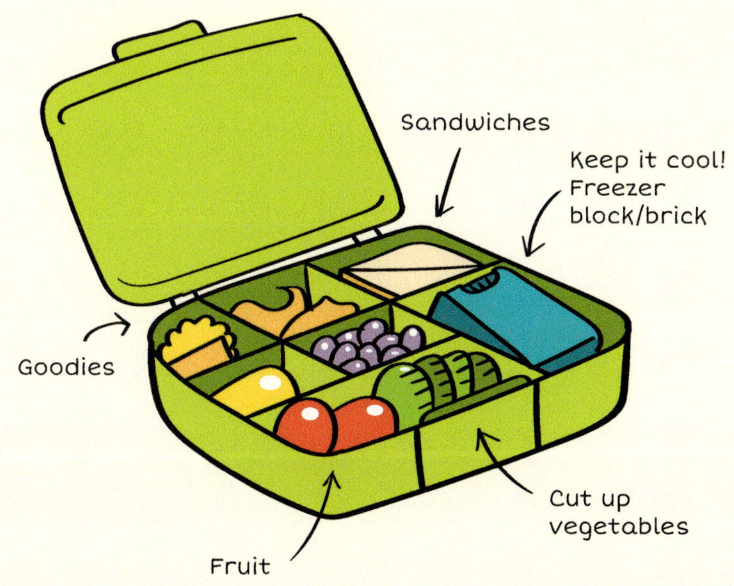

Ideas for your school lunch box

- Carrot, cucumber, celery sticks
- Cut-up fruits (use lots of different **COLOURED** fruits that are in-season)
- Your favourite dip
- Rice crackers
- Cheese sticks or cheese cut into cubes
- Sandwiches cut into small shapes
- Mini sausage and veggie rolls
- Pizza scrolls
- Mini cheese and Vegemite scrolls
- Mini muffins
- Zucchini slice
- Rolled up slices of ham or chicken loaf
- Cherry tomatoes
- Boiled egg
- Falafel balls

Millie says...

At my school, we have what's called 'Munch and Crunch' time about an hour after we begin our school day. During this time, we might eat fruit such as mandarins, oranges, watermelon, apples, bananas or berries. Then we put away our Munch and Crunch and keep going with our lesson. Then we go out to morning tea/recess. I always make sure I drink water at any time during the day, but especially my break times.

My favourite things to pack in my school lunch box are Cruskits (with vegemite and butter), strawberries, blueberries and grapes (my favourite fruits to bring to school). I might take a little lolly for a treat such as a choc-chip cookie or a small chocolate, or even a small packet of Skittles.

I pack my lunch box the night before and then put it in the fridge to put in my school bag in the morning. If I'm taking a sandwich to school, I'll make that in the morning.

Mackenzie says...

At my school, we have recess and lunch. I usually pack a piece of fruit and maybe some cheese and crackers. I eat this at morning tea break. For lunch, I usually pack a wrap with ham, cheese, and avocado. I always take my drink bottle to school. If it's going to be a warm day, I make sure I put lots and lots of ice in it before school. Most of the time, I eat everything in my lunch box, but occasionally I leave some cheese and crackers.

The food pyramid

The **FOOD PYRAMID** can help teach you about what foods you need to eat more of, and which ones to eat less often so you can keep a **HEALTHY BALANCE**.

The three groups of foods you eat from are often shown as a food pyramid.

The top of the pyramid is the smallest part of the pyramid. It contains foods you should only eat sometimes.

The middle of the pyramid contains foods you should eat moderately (a medium amount). They are important for health, but we don't need too much of them.

The bottom of the pyramid is the biggest part of the pyramid. It contains the foods you should eat most of the time.

Based on Nutrition Australia information (www.nutritionaustralia.org)

Drink lots of water

Our bodies are made up of more than 70 per cent water.

We need to ensure we replace our fluids constantly (especially with the lots of running around that happens during the day at school).

TWO LITRES (8 glasses of water) per day is recommended.

Fill a large water bottle with water at the beginning of the day before you go to school. Carry this around with you and drink from it as much as you can throughout the day. For extra flavour, you can add a couple of STRAWBERRIES, or a slice of LEMON or LIME.

School sandwich or wrap filling ideas

Try some of these ideas and combinations

- Honey
- Vegemite, with or without cheese
- Ham, with or without cheese
- Jam
- Shredded chicken with mayonnaise
- Egg and lettuce
- Avocado, with or without Vegemite
- Cheese, chicken and avocado
- Cheese and tomato
- Ham, cheese and tomato
- Salami, with or without cheese and lettuce
- Curried egg
- Falafels and lettuce
- Nutella
- Ham, cheese and avocado

School Lunch Recipes to Try

Over the next few pages are a couple of RECIPES you could make with your parent or helpful adult to include in your school lunchbox.

Make these in batches and you can freeze them for another time.

What are your favourite ideas to pack in your school lunchbox?
Draw them in the spaces below.

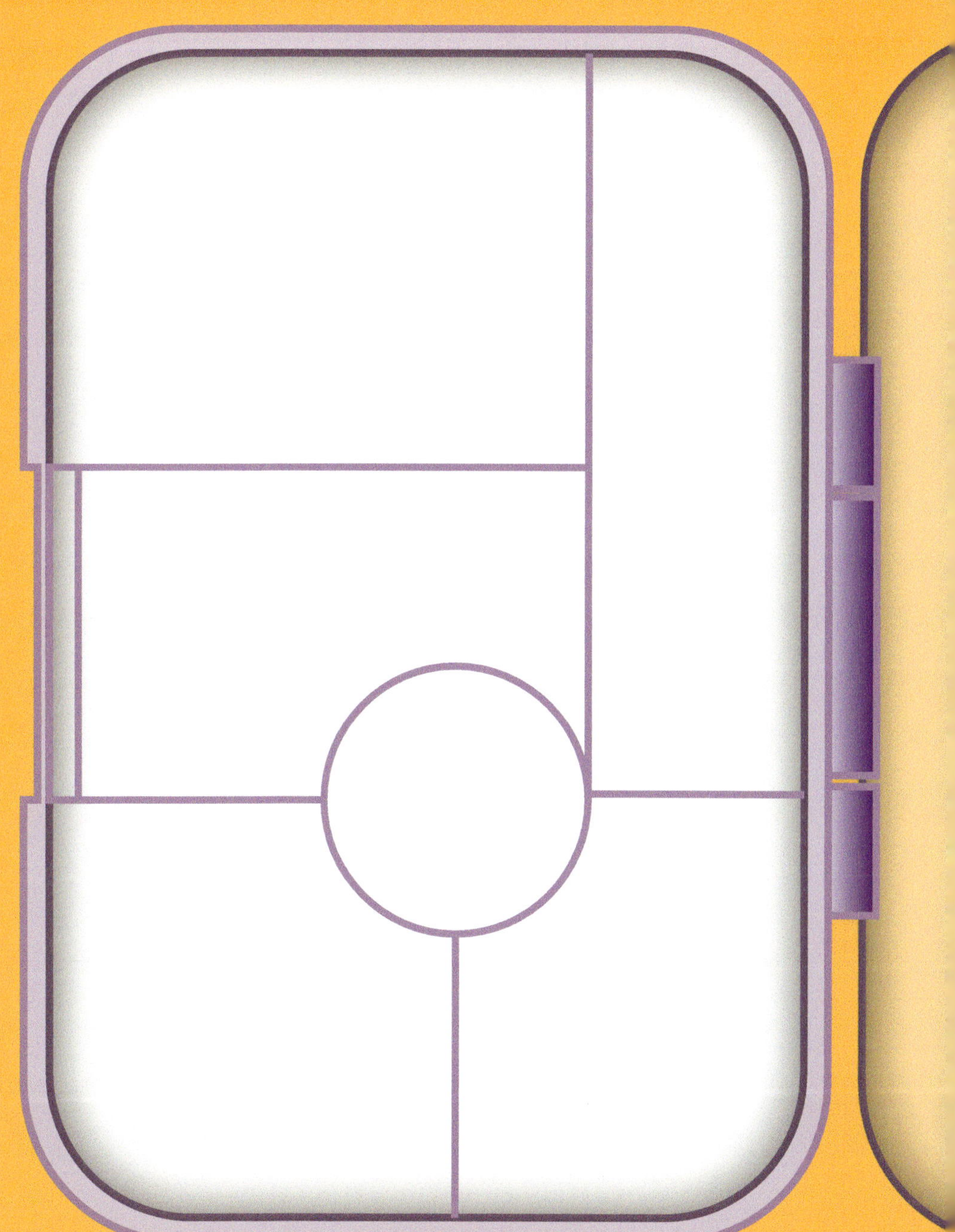

Pizza scrolls

Time Allowance - 50 minutes

What you'll need

- ✔ Frying pan
- ✔ Chopping board
- ✔ Baking trays x 2
- ✔ Wooden spoon
- ✔ Baking paper (so your scrolls don't stick to the tray)
- ✔ Sharp knife (An adult will have to help you chop up the bacon and onion ☺)

Ingredients

- ✔ 1 packet of frozen puff pastry slices (usually comes with 5 or 6 slices)
- ✔ 1 packet of rindless bacon (at least 5 slices)

- ✔ 1 onion (if you want to include onion)
- ✔ 1 small tub of tomato paste/pizza sauce
- ✔ 1 packet of grated cheese

Method (how you actually make them)

JUST 4 FUN

1. Pre-heat the oven to 220 degrees (An adult will be able to do this).
2. Separate and place puff pastry sheet on to the kitchen bench.
3. Chop bacon and onion into very small pieces (you don't have to include onion if you really don't like the taste of it).
4. Place bacon and onion in a frying pan and cook until done.
5. Cover each piece of puff pastry sheet with a thin layer of tomato paste or pizza sauce.
6. Spread a layer of bacon and onion sparingly (this means not too much) over each puff pastry sheet.
7. Sprinkle grated cheese sparingly over each bacon mix.
8. Using an adult to help you, carefully roll one of the puff-pastry sheets from one end to the other (it will be quite full of ingredients) until it looks like a fat caterpillar. ☺
9. Place baking paper onto the baking pans or spray a light layer of baking oil directly onto the pan.
10. Place the caterpillar shaped filled pastry and gently (with help from an adult) slice through into thick sections – see diagram on opposite page.
11. Place each scroll carefully onto the baking tray, making sure you allow plenty of space around each scroll so that they don't get squashed together when they expand in the oven.
12. Bake in the oven for 10-15 minutes until the pastry looks cooked and the cheese has melted.

NOTE: These yummy pizza scrolls can be frozen in freezer bags or containers to bring out the night before you pack your school lunch.

Savoury muffins

Time Allowance - 50 minutes

What you'll need

- ✔ Frying pan
- ✔ Chopping board
- ✔ Muffin trays x 2
- ✔ Wooden spoon
- ✔ Sharp knife (An adult will have to help you chop the bacon and onion.)
- ✔ Large mixing bowl

- ✔ 1 egg (beaten)
- ✔ 2 tablespoons of butter or margarine
- ✔ ½ onion
- ✔ ¾ cup of grated cheese
- ✔ 1 teaspoon of mixed herbs
- ✔ 2 tablespoons of chopped fresh parsley (optional)
- ✔ 1 packet of rindless bacon or fresh chopped ham
- ✔ 2 cups of self-raising flour
- ✔ ½ cup of milk
- ✔ A pinch of salt (optional)

Method (how you actually make them)

1. Pre-heat the oven to 200 degrees. (Ask an adult to help with this.)
2. Grease (or spray lightly with cooking oil) muffin trays.
3. Mix together butter, egg, and milk in the mixing bowl, using the wooden spoon.
4. Add in sifted flour, a pinch of salt, herbs, parsley and grated cheese. Mix these together.
5. Chop bacon and onion finely. (You will need a helpful adult to assist you with this.) Lightly fry these in a frying pan.

   *If not using bacon, you can finely chop some ham.
6. Mix onion and bacon/ham into the mixture in a bowl.
7. Place large tablespoons of mixture into each of the muffin tray spaces. (Make sure you only fill halfway with mixture, as it will rise in the oven as they cook.)
8. Sprinkle some extra grated cheese on top of the muffin mix.
9. Bake in the oven for 25-30 minutes.

NOTE: These yummy savory muffins can be frozen in freezer bags or containers to bring out the night before you pack your school lunch.

Sleep

When you are in school, you need MORE SLEEP than ever because you are having to focus much more during the day. You are also probably being a lot more active at school as well.

Did you know that when you sleep, your body is working hard to RESTORE and REBUILD important cells that help to fight off germs and illness? Your body needs to REBOOT – much like a computer. So you need to give it rest time.

Sleep also gives your brain the opportunity to sort through important and valuable information from your day and file it away for later. Your brain never stops working!

How much sleep do I need?

When you were first born, you probably slept a lot more than you do now. You also would have had a couple of sleeps during the day. Because you are now at school, you need to have between ten and twelve hours of sleep every night. Of course, this might vary depending on how your day went, or how busy your week is. For example, sometimes you might have a special family event during the school week and you go to bed a little later one night. That may just mean that you need to catch up on a little more sleep the next night, or on the weekend.

Try and aim for at **LEAST** ten hours of sleep each school night to allow your mind and body to function at their best during the school day.

What you can do if you are having trouble sleeping

It can be **VERY** frustrating if you are in bed and trying to fall asleep, and you just **CANNOT!**

Here are some **HELPFUL HINTS** that might help you have a better night's sleep.

SLEEP TIPS

- Listen to some calming music
- Pray
- Turn off electronics (such as iPods and iPads)
- Have a warm bath or shower before going to bed
- Read a book for 20 minutes before bed
- Make sure your room is not too WARM or COLD
- Write in a diary for ten minutes about your day
- Have a warm drink

Millie says...

Normally I have a nice hot shower and put my pyjamas on. I then have a bit of a run around to get rid of any extra energy so I will be able to fall asleep. Mum or dad will normally read a couple of books to me when I'm in bed, and then I close my eyes and think of happy things to fall asleep. If I'm having trouble falling asleep, I will get up and run around a bit more, and then I hop back into bed, think of happy thoughts and try again.

If I **STILL** can't fall asleep, I might and go hop into bed with my mum and dad.

Mackenzie says...

When I go to bed at night, I usually like the room to be dark. When I am getting ready for bed, I usually watch a little bit of TV, like an episode of Friends. Then I go and brush my teeth, go to the bathroom, put on my pyjamas and hop into bed. If I'm not feeling too sleepy, I might read for five or ten minutes. If I am having any problems falling asleep, I write all of my **WORRIES** on a piece of paper next to my bed. Then I just rip it up and put it in the bin so I don't have to worry anymore.

SLEEP TIPS FROM...

'I like to read before going to bed.'

Claire, aged 7

'I listen to a podcast.'

Celeste, aged 5

'I read my book and then lie down.'

Sophie H., aged 10

'My mum makes me a special 'sleep potion' which is essential oils, put in a roller bottle and then put on my wrists.'

Madelyn, aged 6

'I'm not really good at falling asleep, but not having a TV or bright lights on and not watching something scary before bed will help. Also, try playing music. Just relax.'

Sophie M, aged 10

'Just be patient and wait until you fall asleep.'

Charlotte, aged 5

'Having a quiet reading time and praying helps me go to sleep.'

Amelia, aged 9

'When I go to bed, I close my eyes and try to think of happy things.'

Lexi, aged 8

'Listen to calming music, close your eyes for 2 minutes without opening, and make sure that you don't use electronics during bedtime.'

Lacey, aged 9

'When I go to bed at night, I put on an eye mask and I also use a weighted blanket. My mum often scratches my head too. This all helps me to have a good sleep.'

Shiloh, aged 6

Exercise

It's important to get a good amount of exercise. When we are **ACTIVE** and get outside, we release the extra energy we have built up, as well as the endorphins in our brain that make us feel happy.

Perhaps you are involved in a local sporting team or club. Or you may just enjoy being outside, running around and exercising with your siblings or friends.

Things you might do to stay active:

- Basketball
- Football
- Skipping
- Tree climbing
- Dancing
- Calisthenics
- Roller skating
- Building cubby houses
- Cheerleading
- Cricket
- Soccer
- Netball
- Athletics
- Gymnastics

Sometimes we can get caught up watching television, spending time online, or playing video games. These activities can be fun, but they can prevent us from getting our bodies moving. So, make sure you build at least **20 MINUTES** of exercise into your daily routine and get moving!

What do you like to do for exercise?

Draw a picture of your favourite activity to help you stay active.

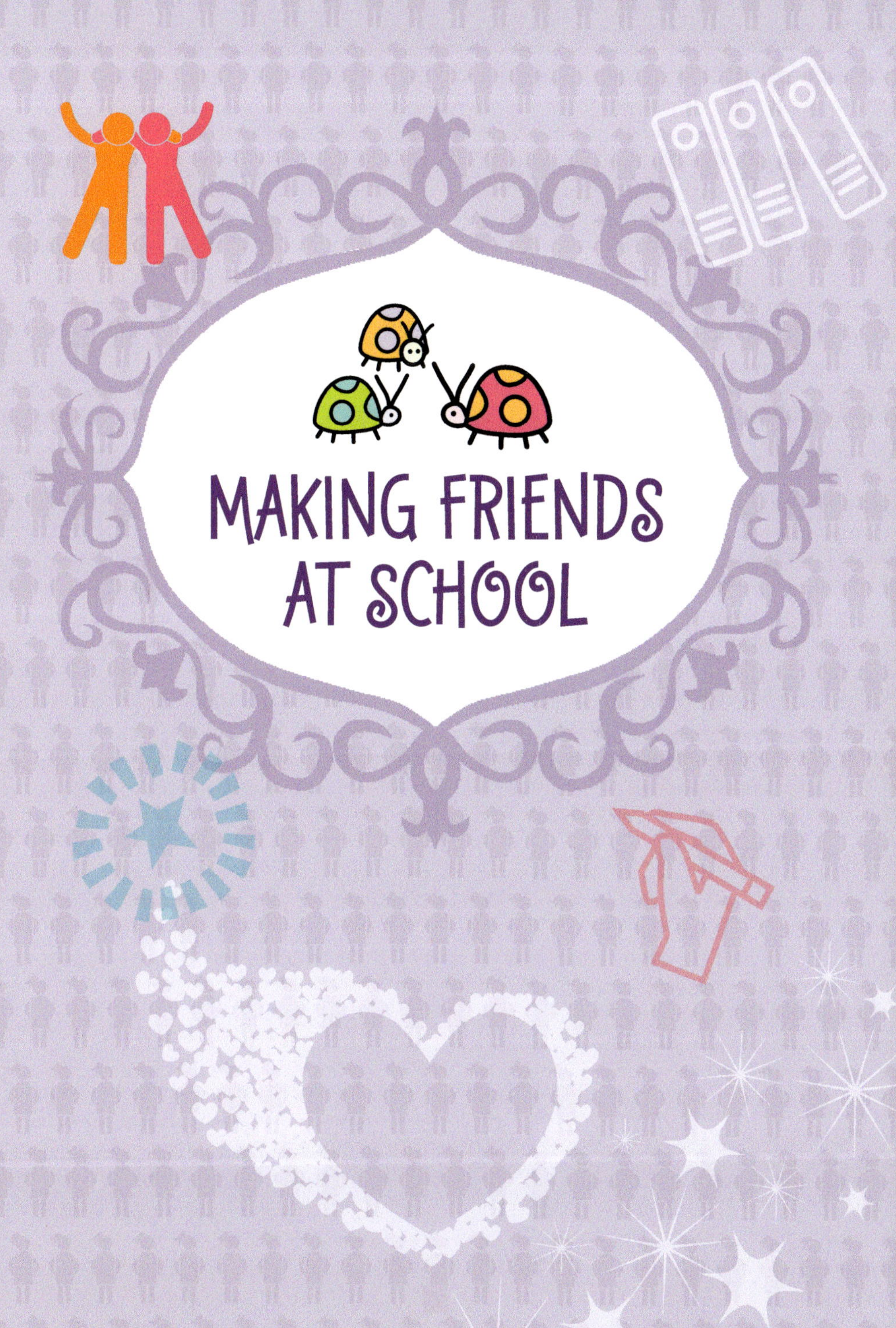
MAKING FRIENDS
AT SCHOOL

Making friends

I actually met my very first school friend when she moved in next door to me. Pretty much from the first time we met we became the best of friends. It helped that we lived next door to each other too, so we could often play together after school.

We started school together in Prep (Reception).

I remember that our teacher was Mrs Bowler. She was tall, friendly, and always smiling. There were nineteen other students in our class. Our school was very small and located in a small country town, but we **LOVED** it!

Our teacher helped us to make friends within the classroom. She would often encourage us to sit next to someone different for some activities, or to play with larger groups of friends during play time. This was great advice for me and my friend too, because it meant that we got to know **OTHER FRIENDS** as well.

Soon after we started school, they built a brand-new school closer to our home, so many of us moved to the new school. There, we had the opportunity to get to know many more friends, as the school was bigger.

A sweet friendship refreshes the soul.
Proverbs 27:9

At recess and lunch we would play games where we would do lots of **PRETENDING**. We would pretend we were from another time, like the olden days, and sometimes we wanted to pretend we were in the middle of a big game with 'goodies' and 'baddies'. We had so much fun that we often felt disappointed when we heard the bell going to come back inside for class.

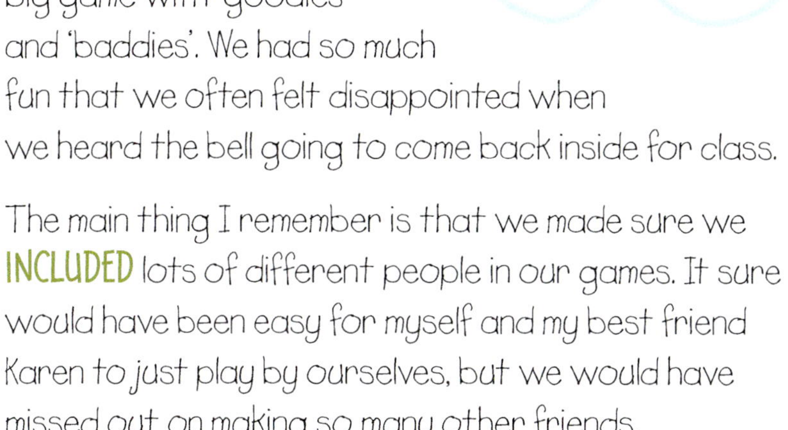

The main thing I remember is that we made sure we **INCLUDED** lots of different people in our games. It sure would have been easy for myself and my best friend Karen to just play by ourselves, but we would have missed out on making so many other friends.

And I **STILL** see some of those friends I made in primary school **MANY** years later. We say hello and smile at each other and remember how much we enjoyed our school years together.

When a friend moves to another school

Sometimes, for many reasons, a friend may have to move to another school.

Perhaps they move away from where they live or for other reasons that you might not understand.

This might make you feel a bit **SAD**, or you might worry that you will **MISS** them terribly. But it doesn't mean you may not see them anymore. Your friend may still live close by, so you can have visits on weekends or over the holidays. If they move interstate, you can write letters and cards to keep in regular contact.

Try to remember, just because you may not see your friend at school every day doesn't mean you can't still be friends. You can still stay in touch. Think about some interesting ways you can still connect.

Dear Claire,
I miss you
being at
school
with me.
I hope you
are enjoying
your new school.
What is your new
school like?
Are you making
new friends?
I have drawn a picture
of my dog Buster for
you.
Miss you,

Sophie x

Making new friends

One of my closest friendships came from the school I teach at. From an early point of meeting, we've just made each other laugh, and laugh! It always felt like the chats and laughs have come so easy. Above all, we respect each other – even if we disagree about something, we stay friends.

Other friends I have formed over the years have come from living in the same street. Almost every day, you'll see a neighbour and say 'Hi'. The more we talk, the more we form friendships.

I've made many friends along the way just simply by being interested in others, smiling when I meet someone new and asking questions to get to know them better.

It doesn't take much to say 'hello' to someone you haven't met before. I am sure I have done this often, otherwise I would have missed out on some pretty awesome friendships!

You will have the opportunity to meet many new friends while you are at school. Some of the friends you make might move on with you to high school (but that's a bit later down the track when you are much older ☺).

How do you make new friends?

One of my favourite quotes is:

> 'The only way to have a friend, is to BE one!'
>
> Ralph Waldo Emerson

What this means is, if you want to make new friends, you have to practice BEING a friend to others. You need to give others an opportunity to get to know you.

I know that this can feel a bit scary for some people at first, but try to remember that just about everyone else is feeling just as NERVOUS and perhaps WORRIED about making new friends as you are. ☺

Millie says...

If I was someone who didn't have a friend at school and was feeling worried, I would look out for another person who seems to be lonely and go up to them and ask them, 'Do you want to play with me?' Hopefully they say, 'Yes please!'

Maybe if you see some people playing soccer, basketball, or any sport, you could just join and pretend you're one of the team mates. ☺

If you are still having trouble making friends, tell your teacher and they might help you find another person to play with.

Mackenzie says...

At my first primary school, quite a few of my friends left for various reasons, so that was very hard for me. Then I moved to a brand-new primary school and made heaps of new friends. I just started talking to others about why I moved schools and talked about stuff I liked to do. I found that we had many things in common. They are now some of my best friends and it's great to be at school with them every day.

Try making friends with children in other year levels. If you have a buddy (a friend chosen for you when you begin a new school) from another year level, you could spend time with them as well.

At first, I was worried about making friends in a brand-new school, but it's not that scary when you give it a try. Just be yourself. ☺

Tips for making new friends at school

'You can make more friends in two months by becoming really interested in other people, than you can in two years by trying to get other people interested in you.'

Dale Carnegie

It's difficult to know how to begin a conversation with someone you don't know very well, or at all. There are some things you can do to let someone know that you would like the opportunity to talk with them...

Be interested

Try and begin a conversation with someone new by showing that you are interested in THEM first. If they are new to your school, you might begin by asking them what school they came from, what they like to do for fun, or how many family members they have. Once you begin asking questions, you are sure to find something in common to talk about fairly quickly.

Use eye contact

This probably seems like something SO SIMPLE but it's something that many girls forget!

Even before you begin a conversation, use eye contact. Look them in the eyes and make sure you nod, smile and look at them when you are talking. When you look someone in the eyes, you know that they have seen you. This is a good thing to do, as it lets the other person know that YOU are interested in talking to THEM!

Smile

When we smile, our entire face lights up. A simple smile says SO MUCH! It says that you are willing to make a new friend. It says that you are happy to talk with the other person. It says that you are interested in getting to know them and that they are VALUED! Most importantly, a smile costs you ABSOLUTELY NOTHING! Come to think of it, you have a never-ending supply of smiles available, so make sure you use them often!

Use a soft, kind voice

When introducing yourself to a new friend, it's a good idea to NOT use your outside yelling voice. Use a gentle, kind voice so that the other person can hear you properly and understand what you are saying.

Ask questions!

When you are first getting to know a new friend (or haven't seen them in a while), make sure you ask lots of questions. Sure, it's great to share your own stories and interests, but also ask questions to get to know the other person. (Have a look at the next page for some ideas.)

Be yourself

The best advice is to **BE YOURSELF!** No one else can be you, and you bring something to your friendship groups that no one else does.

Sometimes, we feel pressure to act like someone else. We can think that our personality is boring and uninteresting – but that's not being real. The problem with not being yourself is that you have to keep up appearances. That means, if you pretend that you really like rock climbing, pretty soon, your friend will want to go rock climbing with you. Or maybe you say you love listening to a certain band. Before you know it, your new friend has just created a playlist for you! And you were just trying to sound impressive!

JUST STOP! The real you is fine and wonderful, and worth getting to know (even if your real hobby is collecting rocks!).

Ideas from...

REAL GIRLS

My tips for making friends are firstly, Introduce yourself.
See if you find a common interest.
Be kind.
Do not exclude other people.
Do not say unkind words.

Annabelle, aged 8

'My advice is to just be yourself, and be friendly.'

Matilda, aged 10

'My best advice is to just be yourself! Also, something that works for me is that I like to be funny, and happy.'

Charlotte, aged 11

'If someone is worried about making friends, I would ask them if they want to come and play with me.'

Sophie, aged 7

'I think that if you are polite, the other person will know that you are friendly and not mean. You can ask if you can play with them.'

Grace aged 9.5

'It's good to make new friends at school because you get to know more people, and then have more people to play with.'

Isabelle, aged 6

'The advice I would give someone for making new friends is just to go for it. Everyone at school is here to make friends, so let your voice be heard, and remember to give everyone a chance.'

Nevie, aged 10

Making new friends

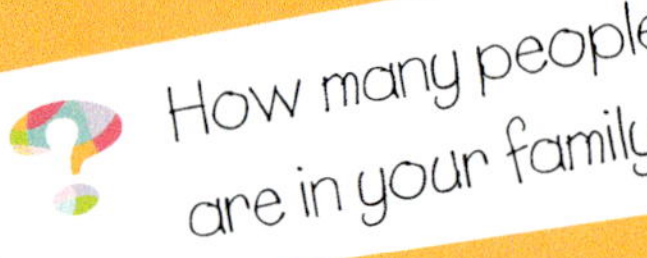

How many people are in your family?

What is the strangest/funniest pet you've owned?

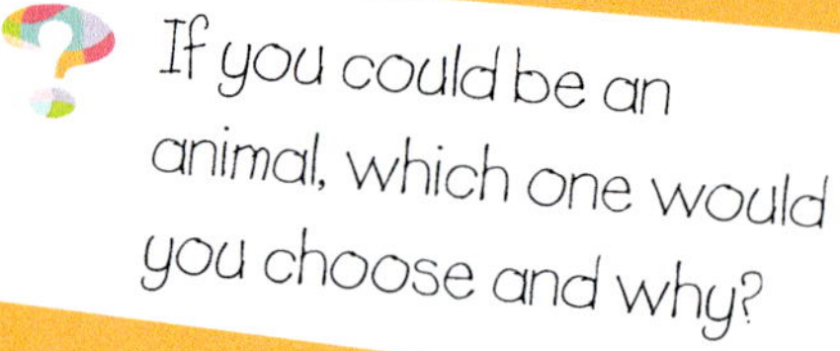

If you could be an animal, which one would you choose and why?

Have you ever met anyone famous?

Have you ever travelled overseas?

How many schools have you been to?

What was your most embarrassing moment?

What is your favourite colour?

Do you play a musical instrument?

If you could have an entire day to do anything you wanted, what would you do?

What is the weirdest gift you've ever received?

What is your all-time favourite movie?

Have you ever been to the circus, and where was it?

What are you most scared of – mice or spiders?

at school...

Questions you can ask a new friend at school

What is your favourite television show?

If you could choose a superpower, what would you choose and why?

Do you have a favourite sporting team that you follow?

Who do you admire most and why?

Is there a pet you wish you could own but your parents won't let you?

What was your favourite birthday you have had, and what made it so special?

Do you have any strange habits?

What would you change about yourself and why?

What special talents do you have?

What is your favourite thing to do on a rainy day?

What do you want to do when you grow up?

Interview some new friends

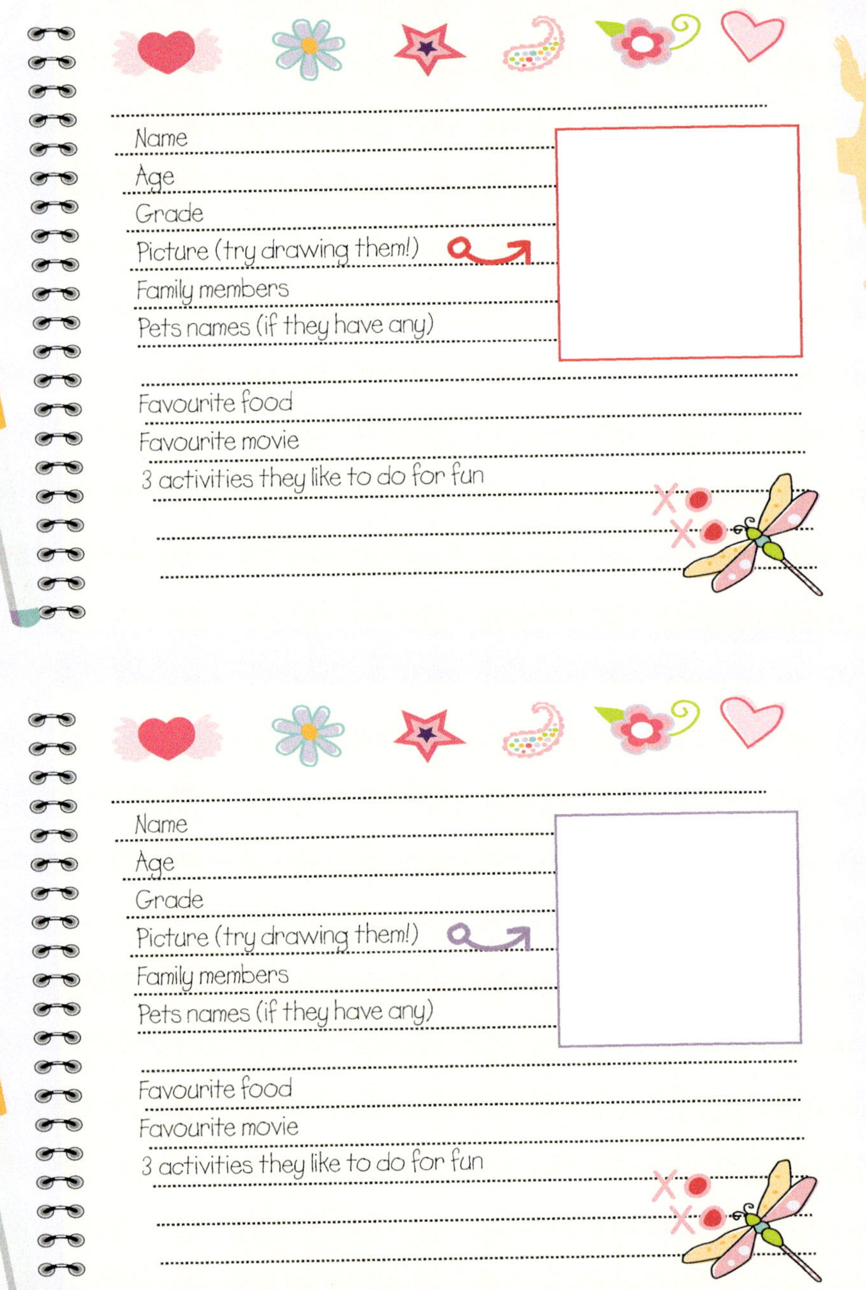

Name

Age

Grade

Picture (try drawing them!)

Family members

Pets names (if they have any)

Favourite food

Favourite movie

3 activities they like to do for fun

Name

Age

Grade

Picture (try drawing them!)

Family members

Pets names (if they have any)

Favourite food

Favourite movie

3 activities they like to do for fun

in your class

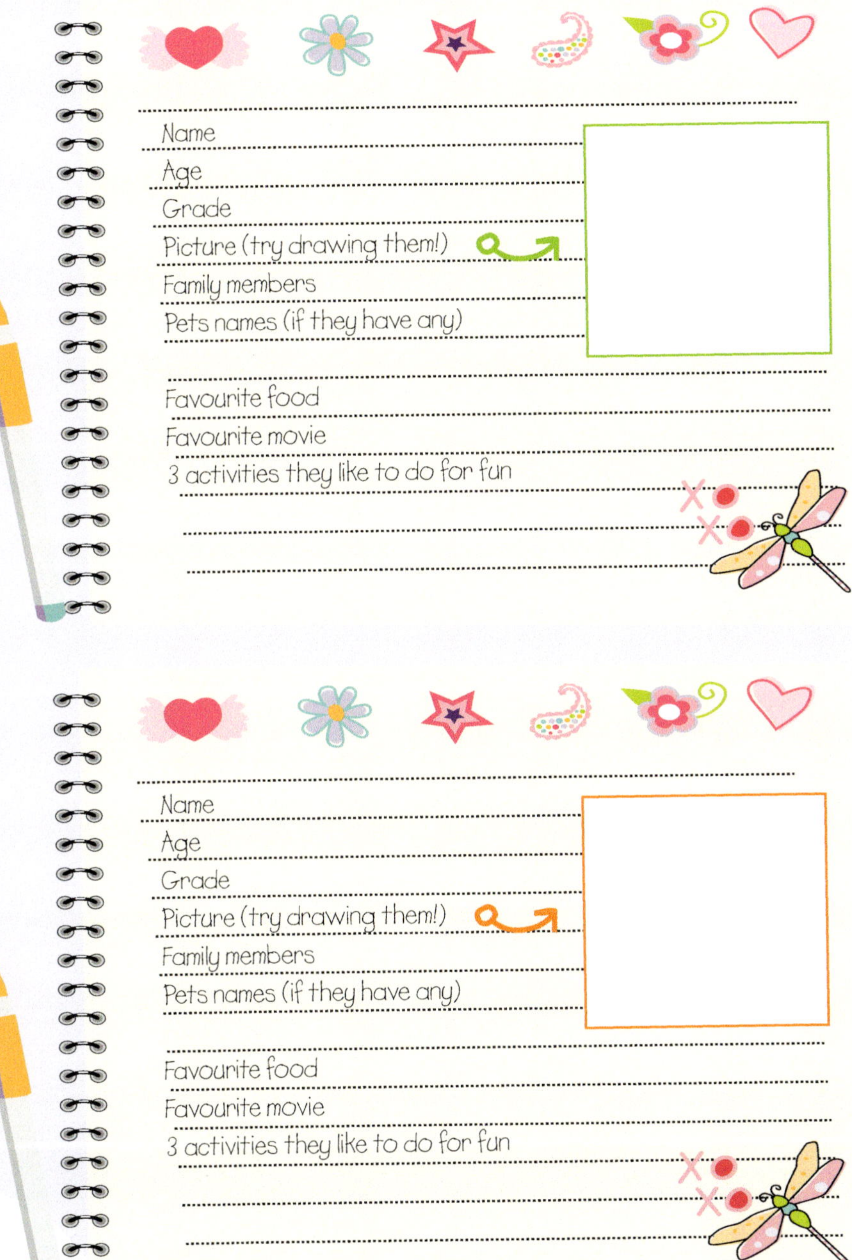

Are you feeling shy?

If you feel a bit **SHY** around others, or find it difficult to go up to a new person and say hello, try not to worry about it. Some girls feel more confident than others when they are at school.

Some girls I know have no problem at all when they are at home with their family where they feel **COMFORTABLE**, but feel shy and worried when they get to school. Please don't worry if this sounds like you. Everyone is different. Do you know that even some teachers feel **SHY** around others? Even famous people you see on TV can feel shy, but can feel perfectly okay when they have to be on camera.

Some ideas to help if you are feeling shy at school:

- Take some big, deep breaths
- Relax
- Smile (this also helps you to relax)
- Choose one person at a time to sit with or play with at recess
- Let your parents or teacher know how you are feeling, and they might be able to help introduce you to a new friend.

What to do if you have no one to play with at recess or lunchtime

'My advice is to ask others if you can play with them, or start your own game and hopefully others will join in.'

Matilda, aged 10

Ask somebody to play with you and say "May I please play with you because I have no-one to play with." You can always play by yourself, or go to the library and read a book. Walk around the playground and collect flowers and leaves.

Annabelle, aged 8

'My advice would be to find a teacher and walk around with them until you find someone else to play with.'

Karlee, aged 9

'Don't be afraid to ask someone if you can join in with their activity.'

Isla, aged 9

'If you see some other kids playing a game you find interesting, go and ask if you can join in. Don't be afraid to ask.'

Abi, aged 10

'Look for another person to play with in the big playground. If they are in a group, ask them if you could play with them. And if you see someone by themselves, ask them if they would like to join in with your game. It's good to care for others.'

Charlie, aged 7

'My advice is to find someone else who seems lonely and you can ask to play together.'

Tara, aged 8

'Try and choose people that have something in common with you.'

Claire, aged 7

'My best advice is to go up to someone you would like to play with and say, 'Hello, can I please play with you?'

Jasmine, aged 7

'My advice is to go up to someone who is alone or maybe someone who might not be alone but who looks nice enough to include you. That's what I do when I'm somewhere with no friends.'

Nevie, aged 10

'If someone was doing a dance or walking around the oval, I would say, 'Hello, could I please join in?' Or if I see someone I know from my class last year, I might say, 'Hello, how about we go and play?'

Grace N, aged 8 (Millie's best friend)

What do you like to do at recess and lunchtime?

'At recess, I enjoy playing sport and talking to my friends.'

Hannah, aged 10

'I like to read a book and go on the swings.'

Matilda, aged 10

'I like to play tiggy at recess.'

Sophie, aged 7

'At recess and lunch, I like to play on the playground.'

Isabelle, aged 6

'At recess, I like to play on the monkey bars, in the special garden in our playground, run around on the oval, or walk around with the yard duty teacher.'

Sophie, aged 6

'My favourite activities to do at recess are play make-believe games (where you can be different characters) and ask your friends different questions such as 'Would you rather...''

Jasmine, aged 7

'Sometimes I play 40/40, which is a game that is a combination of hide-and-seek and tiggy. One person counts to forty and the others hide. It's great fun because the main person has a home base and has to look for people hiding from that base, without moving. If they want to leave the base to look, they have to say, '40/40 off base.''

Mackenzie, aged 10

'Sometimes at playtime, my friends and I just chat. We also pretend play animal games and sister games, or we get out some paper and draw. Sometimes we just play with a basketball or down-ball.'

Abi, aged 10

'I mostly play one bounce, sit and talk, or play on the play equipment. Though the play equipment has been the same for ages and it is getting extremely boring.'

Nevie, aged 10

Learning tolerance

As friends, we all need to learn **TOLERANCE**, because sometimes we will be friends with others who do frustrate us by the way they behave. It can easily get us down. We all need to learn to tolerate others and their personalities. You can't always control who you will spend time with – whether that be friends on your netball or basketball team, or relatives at a big family barbeque. Sometimes, you need to **SMILE** and remember to be interested in what others have to say.

As a side note, being tolerant **DOESN'T** mean you have to put up with behaviour that is unacceptable, such as bullying, gossiping or physical threats. This is **NEVER** okay. But just remember that one day you will be out in the big wide world working in a job, and you can't control the different personalities you will work with. So learning to get along with others and accept that we are created differently is a part of growing up.

You cannot control others' behaviours, but you can always control **YOUR OWN!**

Celebrate who you are!

During your many years at school, you will discover that you have many **UNIQUE** qualities that make you who you are! You will also meet many others who have similar qualities to you, and others who are **DIFFERENT** to you. This is a good thing.

Imagine if we all had the same strengths? For example, if every student had strong leadership skills, it could make it very interesting if you were working on a group project together. Or if everyone was highly skilled in artwork, but no one could come up with exciting ideas, that could also be troublesome.

If you have thoughts and opinions about topics you feel strongly about – **SPEAK UP!** The world needs to hear your voice.

If you have strong ideas and would like to share these, develop your leadership skills. The world needs **STRONG** girls just like you who can show leadership in so many areas of life.

If you love to create, write, paint, draw or make up scripts to perform to others – celebrate these talents! The world needs you too ☺.

BULLYING

Dealing with bullies

For whatever reason, some people find it necessary to treat others with unkindness. Generally, when someone chooses to be unkind or **BULLY** another person, it says a lot more about them than it does about the person actually being targeted.

Often, someone who threatens, teases or is nasty to others, is struggling with their own thoughts of being sad, alone, unloved or having a poor self-image. If they make others **FEEL SMALL** and inadequate, perhaps they will feel bigger and more important.

But bullying others doesn't work that way. The bully ends up looking unkind, small and just plain nasty.

BULLYING HURTS!

It may not necessarily be physical bullying that you are experiencing, but **EMOTIONAL** bullying (being teased, talked about or deliberately left out of games or conversations) can hurt just as much!

What bullying is NOT!

Bullying is not just saying something nasty to someone else e.g. 'Your hair is really ugly!' or 'You're stupid!'

That is simply being nasty. It is not okay, that's for sure, but it's not necessarily bullying. Bullying can be targeted at one person and is often **repeated!**

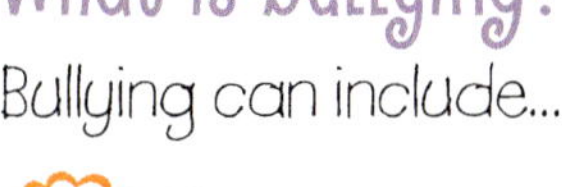

What is bullying?

Bullying can include...

- Hurting someone **PHYSICALLY** (hitting, pulling hair)

- **NAME-CALLING**
- Deliberately **EXCLUDING** someone (leaving them out)

- **GOSSIPING** (talking behind someone's back or making up stories that are untrue)

Usually, these behaviours become bullying when it happens **CONSISTENTLY** (often or all of the time). It can feel like it is never going to stop, and it can leave you feeling angry, sad, alone, confused, scared or distressed.

Here are some things you can do if you are feeling bullied...

Tell an adult

Even if the person bullying you tells you not to tell anyone, you **MUST** let a person know (an adult you trust, such as your teacher or parent) about what is happening. No one deserves to feel scared, intimidated or small because of how someone else is behaving.

Say 'No!'

As soon as you say this single, powerful word – 'No!' – you are letting bullies know – loud and clear – that what they are doing or saying is not okay. If you struggle a bit with this at first, start by saying it under your breath or in your mind until you soon have the courage to say it out loud, with authority. You are worth it! Saying 'No' also lets everyone else around you know that what is happening is not okay. They become witnesses to the bullying and your desire for it to stop.

Stand tall and have confidence

Bullies are looking for people they can steal from. They want your confidence, and they only gain it by taking yours. Try to remember that bullies are really just people who lack confidence in themselves. Bullies try to make others feel inferior to hide their own insecurities.

Don't look the other way if you see someone being bullied.

If you see friends or others being bullied, you need to let someone know. Tell a teacher or your parents what is happening.

Need a bit more information or help?

Take a look at this great website:

bullyingnoway.gov.au

Millie says ...

Bullies are not fun. They might follow you around school and spy on you, or say unkind things about you. My advice is to say to the person, 'Stop it. I don't like what you are saying.' Then just walk away. If they do it again don't react and just keep walking. And if it keeps happening I would go and tell a teacher and ask them to help me sort it out.

Mackenzie says...

If you see that a friend is being bullied, it's important that you stick by them. Ask the person who is bullying your friend: 'How would you like it if someone was treating you this way?' Hopefully they will get the message. If they continue bullying, make sure you go and tell the teacher. They will be able to help.

Bullying is really unkind and hurtful. If it keeps happening tell your teacher or a helpful adult.

GETTING TO KNOW YOUR TEACHER

Getting to know your teacher

When you begin school, you will have a class teacher. They will spend a lot of time with you each day. Teachers are wonderful people. (I should know because I am one. ☺)

Their job is to help you feel **COMFORTABLE** and **HAPPY** at school, and to assist you in solving any problems.

Your teacher will also teach you many new and exciting things like:

- Maths (learning and counting numbers, and adding them together, for example)
- Words (learning what they mean and how to pronounce them)
- Reading

You will have many opportunities in class to create, paint, draw, explore, investigate and learn about so many amazing things.

Remember, it will take **SOME TIME** for you to get to know your teacher, just as they get to know you.

Make sure you talk to your teacher if you are feeling **WORRIED**, **UNSURE**, **UNWELL**, or even if you have just **FORGOTTEN** where something is.

You can also **SHARE** many good and exciting things with your teacher, such as what you did on the weekend, if you got a new pet, or even if you have a new baby brother or sister.

The best thing about my teacher…

'My teacher is really kind.'

Isla, aged 9

'The best thing about my teacher is she is lovely, kind, and caring.'

Sophie, aged 7

'The best thing about my teacher is that she is really nice and does fun things with us.'

Jasmine, aged 7

'I love how my teacher has always supported me with my anxiety. She has been so kind and gentle, and she helped me get over most of my worries. She talks to me and always has time to listen.'

Charlotte, aged 11

'My teacher is really kind, caring, and understanding. She's very friendly and she has helped me and some of my friends sort through some problems.'

Abi, aged 10

'The best thing about my teacher is that she reads us lots of stories.'

Sophie, aged 6

'What I love most about my teacher is that she is always caring and doesn't get too upset if someone does something a little bit wrong.'

Tara, aged 8

'What I love most about my teacher is that she is kind and she speaks with love.'

Isabelle, aged 6

'I like that my teacher is always with me, knows how I'm going, and can always help me improve.'

Nevie, aged 10

'My teacher is really nice. She helps me with my writing and is kind and loving. She is also funny and makes jokes with us.'

Charlie, aged 7

Millie says...

All of my teachers have been really nice. They are always friendly, and they help me with maths, reading and all the activities you need to do around class during the day. If I have any troubles I can always ask my teacher to help me.

Mackenzie says...

My teachers have been really nice and have helped me with my schoolwork or things I have been worried about. Teachers should be a bit strict and only tell you off if you are doing the wrong thing. I love that teachers are not related to you, like your parents, but they are another adult that you see every day who is there to help and support you.

Interview your teacher

You might like to ask your teacher if you can interview them. (Pretend you are a reporter for a newspaper. ☺)

My teacher's name

What is your favourite food?

Have you ever broken a bone before? Where?

What is your favourite holiday destination?

Do you have pets at home? What are their names?

What sports team do you follow?

What do you like to do to relax?

What is the BEST thing about being a teacher?

What is the WORST thing about being a teacher?

Do you have children?

What is your least favourite food?

What is your favourite colour?

What month is your birthday?

What is the best gift you have ever received?

Have you travelled to other countries? Where?

How long have you worked at this school for?

What is your favourite music to listen to?

If you weren't a teacher, what do you think you'd be doing?

SCHOOL DAYS

A typical school day

No day is ever going to be exactly the same at school, but there will certainly be some ROUTINE and STRUCTURE that will help you feel more settled at school.

Firstly, when you arrive at school each day, you will HANG YOUR SCHOOL BAG on the hook provided and bring your BOOKS and PENCIL CASE into your classroom, if they are not already in there. You may also have your READER or other books to return to the classroom.

Your class teacher might begin each school day by having you sit on the floor in front of them, or you may sit at your desk.

The first thing your teacher needs to do is MARK YOUR ATTENDANCE at school (often called marking the roll), because they need to know who is at school on each particular day, and if someone is away ill.

If you are running late to school, which can sometimes happen for a variety of reasons, make sure you check in at the school office or reception so that they can SIGN YOU IN. That way, everyone knows you are safely at school.

Your teacher might begin your morning by telling you what to expect throughout the day, what lessons you'll be having, and any special events that are happening. They might remind you of homework or a notice that needs to be returned. Perhaps it is someone's birthday and they are to be celebrated that day. Your teacher might even sing a song, or even pray with your class.

Different teachers will have many different ways of beginning the day. They will make sure you feel **WELCOMED**, **RELAXED**, and **SETTLED** for the new day ahead.

Different subjects at school

During the school day, you may do many activities that will grow your mind and teach you new skills.

These will include:

 Reading

 Writing

Spelling

 Maths (learning about numbers and fractions, addition, and multiplication)

 Sport / physical education

 History (famous people, such as explorers, inventors and writers)

 Geography (countries, cities, landmarks)

 Science – how life and the universe works (gravity, animals and insects, volcanoes)

 Art (drawing, painting, building, paper mache)

 Music

Homework pouch

Often, children are given a **HOMEWORK POUCH** or **FOLDER** at school which is used to transport your homework, take home readers, school diary, and notices to and from home.

This will be labelled with your name and will be a very important part of being an organised student.

Homework pouch

A word on tests

Throughout your years in primary school, there will be times when you will have tests on many areas of your learning. Some children become very NERVOUS and WORRIED about tests.

PLEASE DO NOT WORRY!

You will have lots of experiences of tests in school, over many years, and they are simply ONE WAY in which teachers can measure where you are at with a whole range of topics and subjects. Teachers are required to gather important information to HELP YOU with your learning. Often, they are able to make adjustments or give you extra assistance in an area of learning by assessing you with your work.

Remember, tests can only give information to your teacher about what you recall on that day at that time. They don't reveal SO many other things you are amazing at, such as being a good friend to others, a helpful student in the classroom, an incredible artist, or a great sport.

School/Classroom Rules

A part of being a member of any community involves following **RULES** or **GUIDELINES** that are created to keep everyone safe and well.

At school, all students need to feel **SAFE** and able to learn at their best.

Your class teacher may begin the school year by discussing some class guidelines with you. They may even ask your class to be involved in creating a set of class rules. These may include:

- Raising your hand when you want to speak in class
- Taking it in turns
- Washing your hands before and after lessons
- Following the teacher's instructions
- Taking care of school property
- Being kind to one another
- Not going out of bounds in the playground

Write some school rules you think would be important to follow...

Before and after school care

Many parents have to work at different hours that may not suit school hours for pick up and drop off. So, some schools offer before and after school care.

You may arrive at school EARLIER than many other students and attend before school care. You may even enjoy breakfast with some other students. Or, you may attend AFTER school care until your parent or caregiver are able to pick you up.

These are run by FRIENDLY and RESPONSIBLE adults. They will often have activities for you to do whilst you attend.

Show and tell

When I was in primary school, I always got excited when it was my day to do **SHOW AND TELL**. This is a time set aside for students to bring in something special from home to share with their classmates. Sometimes, you might even be able to arrange to have a small pet brought in with your parent or caregiver – just for a short time, as part of your show and tell.

If it is something very valuable, you are best to leave it at home, because unfortunately, accidents can happen at school and items can be broken or lost. If you **REALLY** want to bring in a valuable item, ask your parents, or caregiver to bring it in for show and tell, and then take it back home.

Show and tell can be a wonderful opportunity to allow others in your class to get to know you better.

Show and tell ideas

- Favourite photos
- A special ornament
- Favourite books
- Sports equipment
- A small pet (maybe not your goldfish!)
- A special collection
- Special photos in frames
- Awards or certificates
- Art or paintings
- A holiday album
- Special toys
- Things you've built with Lego
- Your new baby brother or sister (with your parent ☺)
- Favourite dress ups

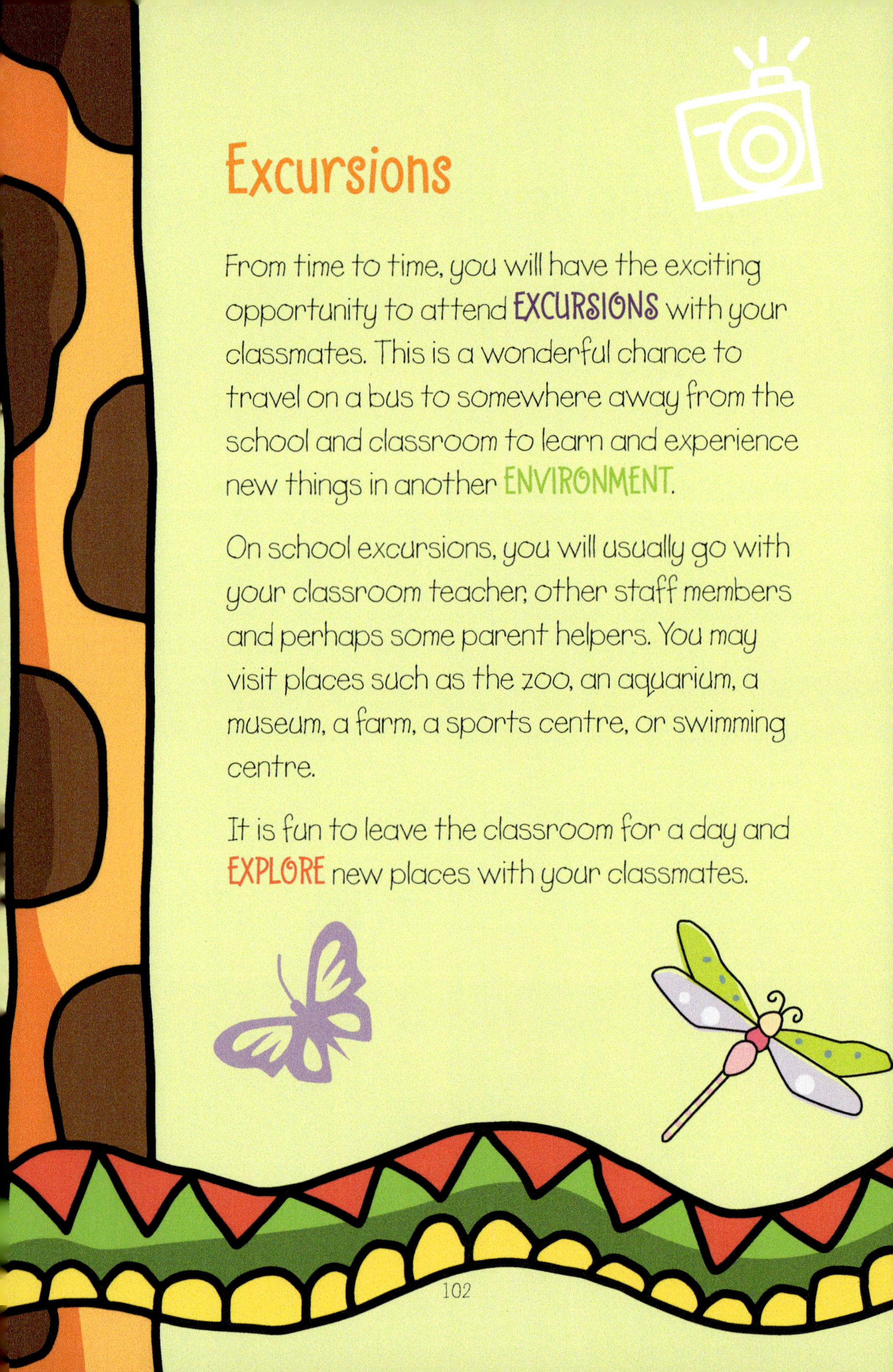

Excursions

From time to time, you will have the exciting opportunity to attend **EXCURSIONS** with your classmates. This is a wonderful chance to travel on a bus to somewhere away from the school and classroom to learn and experience new things in another **ENVIRONMENT**.

On school excursions, you will usually go with your classroom teacher, other staff members and perhaps some parent helpers. You may visit places such as the zoo, an aquarium, a museum, a farm, a sports centre, or swimming centre.

It is fun to leave the classroom for a day and **EXPLORE** new places with your classmates.

Write a story about your favourite excursion or special visitor to school...

School camps and sleepovers

There may be opportunities during your primary school years to go on a SCHOOL CAMP. Sometimes you might start with an overnight sleepover at school. As you move up year levels you may then go on a proper camp with your teacher and other adult helpers.

School camps can be loads of FUN; however, for some children, the thought of being away from home and their family for even one night can be a little SCARY, or make them feel ANXIOUS or WORRIED.

It is perfectly okay if you feel a bit worried about being away from home. Many children, (and even adults!) would prefer to be at home where they feel SAFE and SECURE. However, school camp can be lots of FUN, full of new adventures, new places to see and things to experience. You also have the opportunity to have a sleepover with some of your friends from class.

Your teachers will make sure that you have everything you need to ensure that you have a fun experience on camp. They will send home a notice to your parents or caregiver so that they know exactly where you are going, for how long (usually one or two sleeps) and what you will need to bring.

If you are concerned at all about going on school camp, make sure you talk to an adult. It might be helpful to take along your favourite teddy or a photo with you – something that reminds you of home.

What to bring on camp or school sleepover

- Your pillow
- Sleeping bag or other bedding (some camps provide these)
- Your favourite teddy bear or photo from home
- Bath towel
- Hair brush
- Toothbrush and toothpaste
- Small bottle of shampoo and conditioner
- Soap
- A warm waterproof jacket (for winter)
- Bathers and towel (if you are swimming)
- A few changes of clothes – tracksuit pants and jumpers
- Underwear and socks – several pairs
- A change of shoes
- A small day pack with snacks, lunch and water bottle

Leave electronic devices at home. You don't need these on school camp. Your teachers will always have a phone and can call your parents or caregiver if you need them.

What if I feel sick while I'm on camp?

If you **FEEL SICK** while you are away from home, make sure you tell your teacher, parent helper, or other helpful adult. Make sure you tell them exactly what is wrong. Sometimes you might just feel funny in your stomach because you are **NERVOUS** or **WORRIED** about being away from home. That's perfectly okay too. ☺

Sometimes, just talking about how you are feeling can help settle those pesky butterflies in your tummy.

If at **ANY** time you are feeling unwell – even if it's in the middle of the night – it is okay to get up and tell the teacher or adult that is taking care of you. That's exactly what they are there for.

Other things you can do

- take a few deep breaths
- try and relax
- tell an adult how you are feeling (they will know best how to help you)
- think about how you'll soon be back home again with lots of **NEW MEMORIES** about your **ADVENTURES** on school camp.

Handling wobbly days

Every single person occasionally has a **WOBBLY DAY** (even teachers do!)

Many things can cause a wobbly day. For example, perhaps you didn't get a good night's sleep. Maybe you left an important book at home that you wanted to bring to school. You may have been feeling a bit unwell, or fussy, or unsocial. Maybe, you found it **REALLY** difficult to concentrate in class today, or perhaps you were having some problems with friends.

Everyone, no matter who they are – can have **WOBBLY** days. These are days when it seems that nothing is going right. You may notice adults have them sometimes.

If you are at school, and you **KNOW** you are having a wobbly day – it's okay to tell your teacher.

The things to remember is this:

TODAY WAS JUST A WOBBLY DAY.

And when you lay your head on your pillow tonight, you will fall asleep and you get a brand-new day to begin again tomorrow.

And you can expect that tomorrow will be just **FINE**.

What can you do on a wobbly day?

When I have a wobbly day, I make sure I do at least **ONE THING** that I enjoy doing. It might be having a warm bath, writing in my diary, or watching my favourite movie or television program. Or I might go on a walk with my dog. Often, I just make sure I go to bed early so that my mind and body have a **GOOD REST**.

Write some things you could do if you have had a wobbly day?

Can you recall a time that you had a wobbly day?

What did you do to make yourself feel better?

HOMEWORK

Why do we have homework?

When you are in the first few years of primary school, you may have small amounts of **HOMEWORK** to take home to complete.

Homework is given for a few reasons:

- to help you practice your **READING**
- to help you learn your **SPELLING** words or practise
- **MATH** problems
- to **FINISH OFF** a task not completed at school.

Mostly, homework is set to help you to practise things you learn during the day in class. The more we **PRACTISE** a skill, such as learning to read and spell words or adding up numbers, the better we become at it.

Homework shouldn't take away from your play time and time with your family. It's best to find a time that works best for you and your family to get your homework done.

You may not have homework given to you very often at all, and that is okay. Every school is different, and every teacher is different – they may have other expectations of you.

Homework tips:

- Find a comfortable, well-lit area to do your homework, such as the dining table.
- Have a cup of water and maybe a healthy snack with you, such as some cut up fruit.
- Set a time to complete your homework – it is not meant to take hours! If you are spending too much time on your homework, your parent can let your teacher know that it is too much.
- Have everything you need with you – e.g. pencils, eraser, worksheets, books.

What should I do if I don't understand my homework?

If you are having any trouble with your homework or don't understand what to do, ask a parent or your carer to help you (not to do it for you! ☺). You might also have a big brother or sister who can help you.

Don't **WORRY!** Just do what you can, and ask a parent or caregiver to write a note to your teacher explaining that you are experiencing trouble. Lots of children find homework challenging at times.

Remember, when your teacher knows and understands that you are having difficulty, they can help make a **DIFFERENT PLAN** for you, so that you can have success!

Just do your best!

Millie says...

If I don't understand my homework, I usually ask my mum or dad to help me. I also know that I can let my teacher know if I am having trouble understanding. Recently, my parents organized a tutor for me. This is an adult or older teenager that can give you extra help with your school work. At first, I was worried what others might think, but actually, no one really cares. And it has been a big help for me.

Mackenzie says...

In Grade 5, I get a LOT of homework. Usually I have two spelling activities to complete at night, plus a worksheet of maths. Every night at 5 o'clock, I set aside time to complete my homework. Usually I do it in our study, or the family room. If I'm having any trouble with my homework, I ask my mum to help me. If I am really stuck, I talk to my teacher the next day and ask her for help. My teachers are helpful and help me to understand it better. If I forget to do my homework (this doesn't happen very much to me ☺), I usually have to stay in for half of recess or half of lunch time to get it done, so it's best to get it done at home.

If you have trouble understanding your homework, you could: ask questions, ask a grown-up, or ask a teacher. Do not guess. Don't feel bad because we all sometimes don't know things.

Annabelle, aged 8

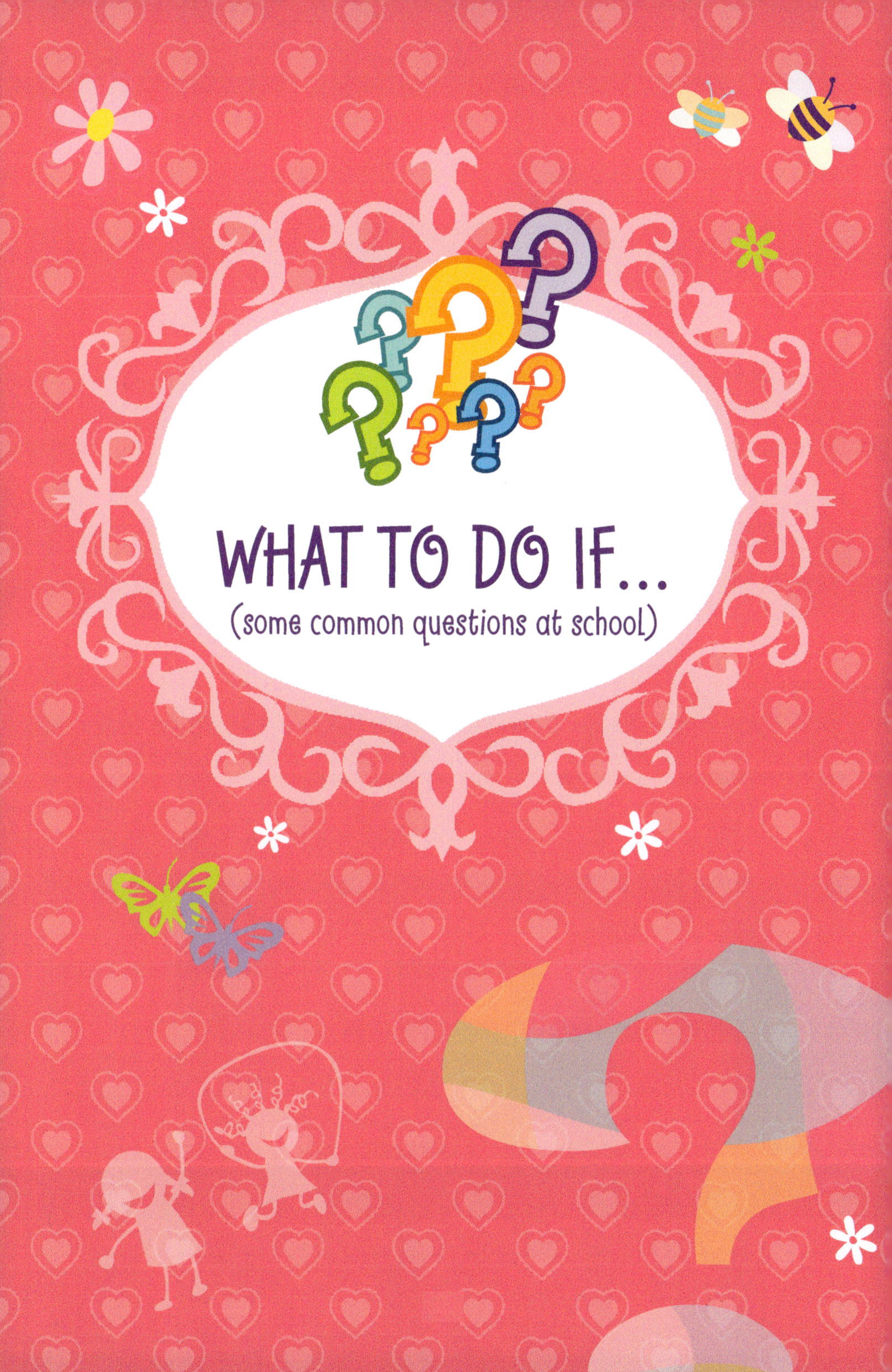
WHAT TO DO IF...
(some common questions at school)

What to do if . . .

You are feeling sad or worried at school

If you are feeling SAD or WORRIED at school, make sure you tell your teacher. Your teacher may ask if you know what it is that you are worried about. Make sure you try to explain as best you can. Your teacher can help you better if they understand the full story and can offer some helpful support and suggestions.

You don't understand the work

There may be many times during your school years that you feel a bit confused or don't understand the work that you are doing in class.

School is for learning but you may not understand everything that your teacher explains.

I remember when I was at school, sometimes my teacher would have to explain how to complete a maths problem, or how to pronounce a tricky word, twice, three times or even MORE.

Don't ever worry about appearing silly if you don't understand something. The best thing you can do is ask your teacher to explain it again, and if you still don't understand, smile and ask again! Sometimes, you may want to ask a friend or a classmate to explain it to you. There is always someone around to help.

Other things you can try if you have trouble understanding...

WATCH Use eye contact – watch what your teacher is doing (try not to be distracted by items on your desk or things going on around you).

LISTEN Listen to what your teacher is saying and try not to talk while your teacher is giving instructions.

ASK Ask for help if you don't understand instructions, and keep asking until you do!

You've forgotten your lunch box

If you get to school and realise you've left your lunch box at home, **DON'T PANIC!** Tell your teacher – they can ask the lovely people who work in the school office to contact your parent or carer who may be able to drop it off at school. Or they may be able to organise an alternative from the canteen, such as a sandwich.

You lose an item of clothing or toy at school

Many children lose all sorts of items at school. That is why we encourage you to **LABEL EVERYTHING** clearly with your name. It is very common for items of clothing to be left out in the playground, in another classroom, or in the gym.

Most schools have a designated area especially for LOST PROPERTY. It's a good idea to check the lost property first if you lose an item of clothing.

It's also a great idea to try and think back to the last place you might have been wearing that piece of clothing. There's a good chance that it is still there.

Finally, make sure you tell your teacher if you've lost something (and your parents or caregiver too). Usually, if a few people are on the lookout for your jacket, hat or jumper, it will find its way back to you – especially if it has your name on it!

* Don't bring valuable items to school!
Leave them safely at home. ☺

Someone takes something of yours

Sometimes at school, items that are important to you may go MISSING. That is why it is important that you have your name on all your possessions.

However, sometimes friends or other students may make a choice to borrow or even take an item of yours without asking you.

It is **NOT** okay for another student to take an item of yours or to go through your school bag and other personal things. If this happens to you, let your teacher know and they will help you work this out.

If one of your school mates takes something of yours without asking you – such as your favourite pen, coloured pencils, book, ruler or food – you need to let them know, gently, that this is **NOT OKAY**.

Approach your friend / classmate and try this:

> *"Jessica, it's not okay for you to take my pencil case without asking me. It is good manners to ask me first if you can borrow my things. This gives me the chance to say yes or no. Next time, please ask me."*

If an item of yours has gone **MISSING**, and you don't know where it is, have a good look around before accusing someone of taking it. Check your locker, school bag, and under your desk again, just to make sure it isn't you who has misplaced the item.

If you **STILL** cannot find the lost item, let your teacher know. Sometimes in my own classroom, a student will come up the front to let me know that they have lost something – like a workbook, ruler or pen.

Sometimes, I ask the entire class to check their own things and take a look in their locker, just in case they took the item. Mistakes **DO** happen, especially when there are many books and stationery items in the classroom at the one time.

Remember, your teacher is there to help if you can't solve the problem first by yourself. ☺

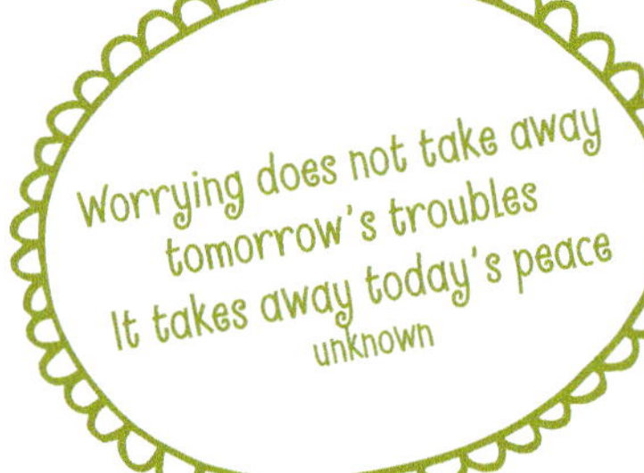

You are missing home

When starting school for the first time, you may feel a bit sad and miss being at home with your parents. You may also be missing your friends from kinder if they haven't joined you at your new school.

Remember, starting primary school is a **BIG** change for you, and it is quite normal that you might be missing your parents or carer during the day.

Perhaps you can put a **PHOTO** of them in your school bag to take a look at during the day, or ask them to write you a little **CARD** that you can read when upset.

If you are feeling sad, quietly let your teacher know. He or she will be very used to other children feeling like this at times. You may not be the only one!

Your teacher might help you feel better by giving you a hug, finding something you can do to take your mind off how you are feeling, and finding some friends you can sit with to help you feel better.

Tell your parent or carer that you felt sad and missed them. They might have some other suggestions.

You get hurt in the playground

There will be times when you are busy playing in the playground, climbing on equipment, running around, playing chasey, and an accident happens (just like they do at home).

If you get hurt, or have any problems while you are in the playground at recess or lunch time, look for the teacher or adult helper that is out on YARD DUTY. Usually, they will be wearing a brightly coloured vest.

If you can't find the yard duty teacher, take a friend with you up to the first aid room or the school office. They will be able to help you get the medical attention you need. ☺

You miss days of school

There will be times when unfortunately, you will get sick and won't be able to attend school for a day or more. You may feel worried or anxious that you will miss out on learning something important and feel behind on your work when you get back to school.

Please try not to **WORRY** about missing school if you are ill. Firstly, you **MUST** stay at home to **REST**, and let your body recover.

Secondly, staying away from school for a few days when you are unwell will also help to ensure that you don't pass on your illness (if it's contagious) to others.

DON'T WORRY! YOU'LL BE BACK WITH YOUR CLASSMATES AGAIN IN NO TIME.

There are also other events that might happen in the life of your family that may mean you have to take a day or more off from school. This might be when you have a **SPECIAL EVENT**, like a wedding, or a special family holiday. Your parents should let your teacher know when this happens. If it's more than a few days, your teacher might make some arrangements with your parents to have you catch up on some important work missed at school.

DEVICES AND THE INTERNET

Internet use and being safe online

The internet is a wonderful place, filled with endless **INFORMATION**, **ENTERTAINMENT** and ways to **CONNECT** with your friends and family from all around the world!

Whatever age you are right now, I am sure that you know all about the internet, and will most likely be using computers, laptops and iPads at school and perhaps at home.

Did you know that when your parents were kids, they didn't even have the internet? Or if they did, they certainly couldn't do everything that you're able to do.

Ask:

- When you were my age, did you have computers?
- When did you use a computer for the first time?
- How did you communicate with your friends before the internet?
- When did you get your first mobile phone and what could you do with it?
- What do you think are the benefits of the internet?
- What are some of the concerns you have about me having access to the internet today?

Of the many ways we use the internet, one of the main uses is to find out information. When you're at school and are given a project to do, you will likely be asked to RESEARCH a topic or person.

The easiest way to do this is by going onto your device and looking it up in the search engine. But before the internet, children just like you had to go to their school or local public libraries to find books about that topic and take notes from there.

Some homes were lucky enough to have a collection of books called the 'ENCYCLOPEDIA'. These books had thousands of pages that had information about any and every topic! But with the world changing as quickly as it is today, these encyclopedias have become outdated.

If we use the internet to research a topic, it's important to use websites that are **OFFICIAL WEBSITES**, not just written by a person with an opinion.

Did you know that it's very easy for a random person to build a website and write facts that may not be correct? While researching on the internet can be very informative, we must always remember to check that the website comes from a trusting source.

Reliable websites

Here are some great websites that are guaranteed to provide you with reliable information for your next school project:

www.education.abc.net.au
www.natgeokids.com/au
www.worldwildlife.org
www.academickids.com

REST AND PLAY
TIME

WORD FIND

S	U	N	G	A	B	L	O	O	H	C	S	R	O	U	T	I	N	E
A	L	S	U	N	H	A	T	F	O	L	K	O	O	B	N	S	T	Y
P	N	O	R	I	E	N	T	A	T	I	O	N	W	K	E	O	E	R
L	O	V	L	E	A	F	R	I	E	N	D	S	H	I	P	S	A	E
A	T	A	R	S	A	T	X	E	T	E	X	C	A	P	L	Y	C	N
Y	I	S	L	L	E	B	E	N	H	I	T	I	C	E	E	A	H	O
G	C	M	R	O	F	I	N	U	S	C	O	S	A	N	R	D	E	I
R	E	Y	O	U	C	T	O	S	N	S	A	S	M	C	A	I	R	T
O	S	N	H	A	R	T	R	U	L	E	R	O	P	I	S	L	Y	A
U	S	E	O	O	S	U	B	J	E	C	T	R	T	L	E	O	E	T
N	R	P	P	H	C	I	H	W	D	N	A	S	G	R	R	H	A	S
D	S	S	S	H	T	A	M	K	Z	O	B	M	O	V	A	L	R	T
L	U	N	C	H	B	O	X	E	L	T	T	O	B	R	E	T	A	W
H	O	M	E	W	O	R	K	Y	H	T	L	A	E	H	S	U	B	G

Circle these words as you find them (some may be backwards ☺)

camp
sunhat
teacher
playground
book
textas
bell
routine
notices
waterbottle
schoolbag
lunchbox
uniform
maths
sandwhich
year
orientation
friendship
oval
sport
subject
art
homework
bus
pen
pencil
ruler
eraser
scissors
stationery
healthy
holidays

Play

In primary school, you can get very busy – especially if you have out-of-school activities and homework. It's really important that you also have TIME TO PLAY! Even teenagers and adults need to make sure they schedule in time to do things they ENJOY.

What things do you like to do when you play?

Perhaps you enjoy building CUBBY HOUSES, making SLIME or building things with LEGO.

When I was in primary school, I loved to play dress-ups, create plays with my best friend Karen, and perform these in front of our friends and family. We also enjoyed playing with our dolls, and we would set them up and pretend we were teachers running a classroom.

There were other times when we would set up a picnic in the backyard. If you have a few stuffed animals, you could pretend that you are the owner of a zoo. You could even make special signs for your backyard zoo.

Use your IMAGINATION – Your imagination is AMAZING and can help you come up with many different play ideas.

Making play dough

Time Allowance - 40 minutes

You'll need a helpful adult to assist with the saucepan on the stove

What you'll need

- ✔ Large saucepan
- ✔ Wooden spoon
- ✔ Small containers or zip-lock bags x 6

Ingredients

- ✔ 2 cups plain flour
- ✔ 3/4 cup salt
- ✔ 4 teaspoons cream of tartar
- ✔ 2 cups lukewarm water
- ✔ 2 tablespoons of vegetable oil (or coconut oil)
- ✔ Food colouring, optional

JUST 4 FUN

Method

1. Mix together the flour, salt and cream of tartar in a large pot.
2. Next add the water and oil. If you're only making one colour, add in the colour now as well.
3. Cook over medium heat, stirring constantly. Continue stirring until the dough has thickened and begins to form into a ball.
4. Remove from heat and then place onto wax paper. Allow to cool slightly and then knead until smooth.
5. If you're adding colours after, divide the dough into balls (for how many colours you want) and then add the dough into small zip-lock bags or small containers.
6. Begin with about 5 drops of colour and add more to brighten it. Knead the dough while inside the bag so it doesn't stain your hands. Once it's all mixed together, you're ready to **PLAY.**

School holidays

The school year is usually divided into four **TERMS**, each lasting between nine and eleven weeks. Then you get to have a couple of weeks break for school holidays.

School holidays give you time out from the busy routine of school and give you the chance to sleep in, catch up with other friends, have play dates, relax and rest.

When summer time comes around, school will be over for the year. This break is **BIG** – up to 7 weeks off school!

This is a good opportunity to have family time and create many new memories. You may even be lucky enough to go on a holiday and travel to another town or state.

If you're at home and feeling a bit bored, try:

- Make play dough (with an adult's help).
- Plant a vegetable garden.
- Write a children's book and create the illustrations.
- Set up a tent outside and have a sleep out.
- Build an cubby house inside using sheets and blankets (ask your parents first).
- Plant flowers in pots.
- Clean out your wardrobe and donate any clothes that don't fit to charity.

More holiday ideas

- Have a cooking day
- Create some artwork
- Reorganise your bedroom
- Print out some favourite quotes for your bedroom wall
- Learn to knit or sew (ask an adult to teach you – maybe Grandma)
- Have a PJ day and watch your favourite movies with some popcorn
- Organise a sleepover with a school friend
- Read a book
- Listen to music
- Make up a dance
- Write a play with friends and perform it in front of your family
- Write a script for a short film and film it in your backyard
- Plan a picnic
- Visit the zoo
- Have a sleepover at your grandparents' house
- Build something with Lego
- Take photographs
- Make a kite out of sticks paper and string
- Colour something in
- Build a volcano
- Make slime
- Bake and decorate cookies
- Lego challenges – build the highest tower
- Take a trip to the local library and borrow books
- Paint a large mural on a canvas
- Choose a spot on a map and ask mum or dad to take you on an adventure there
- Take a trip to the beach
- Go fishing
- Go hiking
- Draw paper dolls and cut them out
- Make sculptures out of clay
- Collect leaves and make artwork out of them

In conclusion

WELL, HERE YOU ARE! You've made it through to the end of the book, and hopefully you are feeling a bit more prepared for starting school – or perhaps you have been given a few more **TIPS** and **ADVICE** to help.

Some of my favourite memories were from my primary school years. And you know what? I **STILL** see some of my friends from my school years, as I go about my life now – and that is over 40 years later. **I KNOW!**

Well, my hope and prayer for you, special girl, is that the friendships you make at school, and the experiences you have, and the challenges you may face and overcome, will impact your life in some wonderful way.

Remember this: Your primary school years have a **LOT** to do with your **ATTITUDE** – how you **FEEL** about school.

Even if it hasn't been such a great experience so far, it doesn't mean you cannot start over again right now and take on some of the advice and ideas in this book.

Take care, and lots of luck to you as you move through the next few years at school.

With love, *Sharon*

Extra special thanks

Special thanks to all the wonderful children that wrote to me and gave me some of their best advice and tips for school. And a **HUGE** thank you to my two amazing assistant authors, Millie and Mackenzie. I **REALLY** enjoyed working on this book with you two **AMAZING** girls. Thank you for all of your input and help into making this book so special. xx

DO YOU NEED HELP NOW?

if you ever find yourself in distress, trouble, and need a helpful adult, you can be in contact **ANYTIME** with Kids Helpline. This is a **FREE** telephone and online counselling service for young people aged 5 upwards.

1800 55 1800

www.kidshelpline.com.au

More cool titles in the GirlWise series...

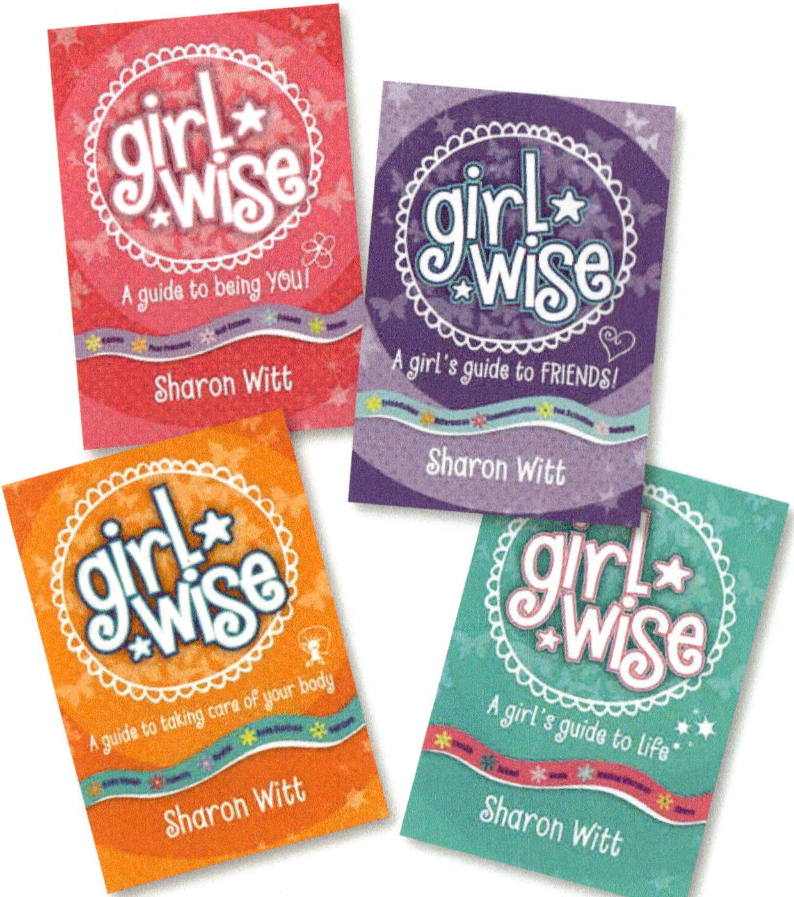

www.sharonwitt.com.au

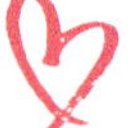

Want to write to Sharon?

You can let her know what you enjoyed about this book.

Email: info@sharonwitt.com.au